—— THE ——
CHASM

Be blessed [signature] 5-9-24

KARALEE RATLIFF

ISBN 978-1-63903-005-7 (paperback)
ISBN 978-1-63903-006-4 (digital)

Christian Faith Publishing, Inc.
832 Park Avenue
Meadville, PA 16335
www.christianfaithpublishing.com

Printed in the United States of America

1

On September 10, Tim decided to take a walk. He was fifty-two and had just suffered the loss of his wife and his mother in a tragic automobile accident. The funeral was two weeks ago, and he had been so consumed with the loss he did not have time to process things on his own. All his kids were right there to help and console and lean on him. They still call him every day (multiple times) to check on him, but Tim needed to escape. He needed to process his emotions. He needed to be in silence, away from the constant ringing of the phone and the doorbell.

Tim and his wife Mary had just purchased this discreet and cozy cabin on five acres of beautiful woodland. They had taken several walks through the trees before the accident and knew that they had made the right choice for their elder years. The town was about five miles away and was equipped with everything they would possibly need. (Extra fun stuff was thirty miles away in the big city.)

Mary had enjoyed the moist and rich soil for her flower plants and vegetable garden. She had also planted a couple of small fruit trees just because. She had told Tim they were cute in the picture and so she wanted them. Tim could never say no to her.

Tim enjoyed the sounds of the brook that separated their property from the neighbor's. You could sit on the back porch and listen to it gurgle in the distance. Though faint, it was very soothing. This morning, with his coffee in hand, Tim opened the back door and sat down in silence for the first time in over a month. He left his cell phone on the charger in the bedroom on the other side of the house and on silent. He turned the ringer off on the house phone and turned the volume down on the answering machine. Tim just wanted silence.

It was about 7:30 a.m., and the sun was just beginning to crest over the eastern pasture. What a sight. As he sat there with coffee in hand, his mind began to drift. The sights he saw at first was the vision he and Mary originally had for this homestead. They wanted a safe place for the grandkids to play and explore. When they were both kids, running around in the woods was as normal as changing your underwear after a bath. Splashing in the creek was the ultimate swimming pool. Climbing trees was the best jungle gym, and traipsing through the woods was the best to expand the imagination. The final decision on this property was also so that they—Tim and Mary—could rekindle their youth as well.

As he sat there drinking his coffee, Tim could see the little ones racing through the yard, diving under the bushes to hide and climbing high into the oak and maple trees to get away from the grizzly bear (older sibling). The screams and giggles of jovial youth melted one's heart. The joy that this place had already brought to their family was insurmountable.

Tim looked down and realized that he needed another cup of coffee. He got up and left this memory for another round of fuel. When he entered the house, he noticed that it was nearing 9:00 a.m. and thought, *Oh wow*. Tim grabbed another cup of coffee and made himself some toast. He took his breakfast and went back outside to memory lane.

Taking up his spot and seeking out what was going to be his next memory, he saw Mary and him planting the two fruit trees. He was so aggravated that day. The kid at the tree farm was annoying; he did not have a clue what he was doing. Tim was convinced he only got the job because of family connections. Mary had been the business of the purchase because Tim was ready to take the young man out to the nearest tool shed and give him a lesson in manners and professionalism. Mary was able to communicate in a nurturing and motherly tone to this brat who, well, in Tim's mind, needed a lesson or twelve in decorum.

Once they got the trees home, Tim was still reeling over the entire encounter. Mary, who had had enough of Tim's tantrum, picked up a clump of moist dirt and started a mud war with him. At first, he was furious, and then he saw the devilishness in her eyes, and it was game on. What should have taken about an hour to complete took well into the darkness of the evening because there would be a truce and then someone would violate the treaty. By the time it was done, they had to hose themselves off outside before entering the house for a shower.

Tim smiled and cried at the same time.

Wiping the tears from his eyes, he realized that his cup was empty again and the toast was gone. So as not to get into trouble for leaving his plate outside, Tim promptly rose and took his plate to the sink and his cup for another load of fuel. When he placed the plate in the sink, he thought, *Ha, she can't yell at me now, I was a big boy.* He giggled and headed for the bathroom.

Walking down the hall, he glanced in the bedroom and noticed that his phone was dark, but the light on the answering machine looked like it had Tourette's. Glancing down at his watch, he saw that it was going on eleven, and he figured his kids were about to have a heart attack. Tim finished his business and then pressed play on the machine. He was correct; it was all his kids calling to find out why he was not answering the phone. Tim picked up his cell phone, and it lit up like a Christmas tree from all the texts and missed calls. All the messages were the same.

"How are you doing? Where are you? Why aren't you answering your phone?"

To settle the savage beasts, Tim made a group text and explained he was having a day to himself. Do not worry, he was just drinking coffee and walking down memory lane. He did not want to talk to anyone; he just wanted silence.

Tim grabbed his third cup of coffee and went back outside. He also grabbed a cushion for the chair because it was not as comfy as it was first this morning.

This morning's trip down memory lane brought back the very reason he and Mary had purchased this place. Several memories came gushing back. Jon, the oldest, loved to sit under the elm and daydream. Margaret would run like a wild child for hours and battle the evil forces of the world. Janey liked to splash and play in the creek. Todd would create other worlds to annoy Janey. All of them would gather and build forts and complex cities with leaves, sticks, and logs. (It was a bear to mow when they were done.) The family would take long walks through the woods and look at all the wonders of the universe. The best part was when Tim and Mary bought the place, the kids were already older, and it did not bother them to leave the hustle and bustle of the city. They too were ready for a simpler place for freedom.

Tim spent the entire day walking down memory lane. Two pots of coffee, a couple sandwiches, lots of tears, but for the first time since the accident, Tim felt peace. Later in the evening, he called each of his kids and explained his day. They each were relieved he was okay and that he had a good day. Each laughed and cried with their father over the different memories. Tim told them that he was going to go "off the grid," with no cell phone tethering him to the outside world for the next couple of days but promised that, by eve's end, he would call them and let him know about his day. He explained that he just needed to escape and enjoy and maybe even scream for the loss, but he needed to be alone. The kids understood and promised to try and be good…but there was no guarantee. Tim laughed and bid them each a good night.

Over the course of the next couple of weeks, Tim would set out for a new trip down memory lane. Some days, it would consist of walks through the woods, some days it was simply sitting in his easy chair staring out the front window and watching the squirrels play in the yard. Each day was refreshing and haunting at the same time. Tim knew he needed to do something or he was going to get stuck in a rut of nothing, and he knew that Mary would come back and kick his tail if he allowed that to happen. But what could possibly be a good something for him to do?

Tim had retired early when his company offered him a nice settlement to leave. The life insurance had paid off the house, so his only expenses were the utilities. He had no place he had to go, so it was up to him to figure something out. His mind wandered to trips of travel, but nothing sounded like something he was ready for. He thought about a part-time job in town, but why would he want to get up early if he did not have to? As his mind muddled through the endless possibilities, he realized that almost all the memories he was reliving were of the "noise" of the playful nature of the property. He needed to play. But…who to play with. That was now the question.

As he sat one Saturday afternoon in his workshop sipping his Coke, he felt the urge to build a birdhouse or something. But he didn't want to do it alone. He wanted to build new memories, and he called Janey to see if Timmy, his namesake, could come over and play. After she giggled at the idea, she said she would ask the little feller if he wanted to go play over at Grandpa's house.

Tiny Tim and Tim had a special bond from birth. But when Mary died, Tim got lost in the grief. Tiny did not understand why Grandpa was acting this way and had told his mother on several occasions that he wanted to go visit. Tiny was now seven and had a lot to share.

Janey found Tiny out in the backyard digging for pirate treasure in the sandbox. He had already found several gold doubloons, artifacts from an ancient Cherokee nation, and a cat turd.

"Tim, Grandpa is on the phone."

Tiny's head sprung up like a spring shooting out of a pen. "Grandpa!"

"Yes." Her smile from his excitement consumed her face. "He wants to know if you can come over and play?"

"Can I, Mom, please?"

"If you want, yes you can. Let me see when he wants you to—" Before she could finish her sentence, Tiny was in the house getting cleaned up and his belongings together to take to share with his best pal.

"Dad, Tiny is already packing. Ha-ha! So when do you want him there? I can drop—"

Tim interrupted, "I am pulling into your driveway now."

Janey just shook her head as she was like, "These two kids."

Tim got to the door, and Tiny was running out of his room screaming, "GRANDPAAA." He dropped his bag and tackled Tim at the waist, who fell to the floor like he had been hit by a tank. Tiny laughed at his Grandpa's antics.

Janey just stood back and let the two juveniles wrestle. Tim asked if Tiny could spend the night because he had a big project he needed his help with. Tiny's eyes lit up and flipped his head around to his mother with a begging look of "please say yes." Janey could not say no and told Tiny to go pack a bag for overnight.

Up in an instant and back again, an overnight bag was packed and ready to go. The boys loaded up in the truck, and off they went. Janey was teary eyed as they pulled out of the drive knowing that each of these boys needed this more than ever.

Tim pulled into Frankies Burgers, because men must eat. They had a major job ahead of them, and they were going to need all the energy they could muster. (Frankies was Tiny's favorite place to eat.)

As they sat in their favorite booth, Tiny began a series of tales that happened in Tim's absence. Totally engrossed in each story, Tim listened to each and every detail and asked specific questions to make sure of his clarity of the story. He also added a few weird questions to get Tiny to slow down long enough to think and then tell Tim that he was foolin' with him.

The boys finished their lunch and headed for the house. When they arrived, Tiny took his bag and ran to his room and threw the bag in the door and back out again to where Tim was just getting the groceries from earlier out of the truck. Tiny grabbed a couple bags to help, and in the house they went. Tim told Tiny that he wanted to build a birdhouse but needed a man to help him with the hard stuff. Tim asked Tiny if he could be that helper. With pure excitement, Tiny said he could but asked if they could take a walk in the woods first. He missed the woods. Tim could never say no to this boy, and off they went.

Walking alongside each other, Tim and Tiny made up stories of adventure that must have taken place before all the people showed up and messed it up. Bands of robbers hiding in the trees, Indians lurking behind every bush, bandits jumping out and robbing unsuspecting travelers…and the list went on and on. As they approached the brook, Tiny found a rather large rock and climbed up to the top, turned around, and began his lecture of the forest.

"You see, weary traveler, these woods were once occupied by a group of people called…" he paused for a minute, smiled, and continued, "a people called the turds."

Tim laughed. "The turds?"

"Yes, young man, the turds. Now don't interrupt. It's rude" Tim apologized, and Tiny continued his story.

"The turds, you see, were a group of people that were kicked out of town because they did not like to take a bath. The town people all agreed that they stunk so bad that they smelled like turds, and that is how they got their group name. The turds did not like that name and did not like the town people for calling them that because, you know, name calling is not nice. So the leader of the turds was George, and he liked to be called George of the jungle, and he rode a cheetah everywhere he went, like a skateboard. George's girlfriend was Gabby, and she had a pet warthog."

As Tiny produced this most entertaining story from atop his rock and in full animation, Tim smiled and laughed at each new idea this small but stout seven-year-old could come up with. His imagination seemed to be endless.

"George and Gabby had two friends, Twinkie and Ding Dong (Tiny's favorite treats). These four people were the turds. You see, young traveler, they were so upset at the town people that every time one of the town people came to the woods, they would jump out from behind the bushes and trees and rock, knock them to the ground, roll around on top of them, and then kick them in the butt. That way, they smelled like turds too."

Tiny jumped down off his rock, and to the brook he went. Tim just laughed and shook his head. Tiny was so happy about his story. He told Tim that the Turds got tired of smelling bad, so they took a bath in the brook, and it took so much water to get them clean; that is why the brook doesn't have as much water as it did back then.

Tim belly laughed, and the two continued on their travels. They splashed and played and had a great time. Tim had grabbed a couple of snack bars and bottles of water just in case they were gone a bit. As they came to the bridge, Tim asked if Tiny was ready for a snack. They sat down on the bridge with their legs dangling off the edge.

Tim got the snacks out and ready, and the boys watched the brook gurgle beneath their feet.

"Grandpa?"

"Yes, son."

"Are you happy?"

Taken aback by the boy's question, Tim replied, "Yes, I am happy. Why do you ask?"

Tiny took a big bite of his bar and said, "Mell, uh, mgghg, uspdt."

Tim smiled and said, "Would you like to try that again without food in your mouth please?"

With a food-filled smile, Tiny nodded his head, then he said, "Well, you seem upset. Like, very sad upset. Is it because Grandma died?"

Tim could hear the sincerity and love of concern in the boy's voice. Genuine concern emitted from his eyes as he sipped his water.

"Yes, I am sad. I miss your grandma very much, but I am trying to be happy again. That is why I asked you to come over. I am always happy when you are here."

Tiny smiled, nodded, and leaned over to rest on Tim's side. As he finished his snack, Tiny asked, "Grandpa, is Grandma with God?"

Taken aback by the question, Tim answered, "I suppose she is. Are you ready to start walking again?"

"Yep," and up he jumped. He handed his bottle to Tim, and the adventure began again.

By the time the boys got back to the house, it was time for dinner. There was no time to work in the shop; they needed to get dinner moving along. (Tiny informed Tim of the time for he had learned how to tell time in school, and he knew.) The boys decided that it was a manly hotdog night with manly potato chips (brats and Doritos).

After dinner, the boys did the dishes and thought it would be a good time to go out to the shop to get things together for the birdhouse. They needed to make sure they had all the supplies they would need for their project. They wanted to make sure they had all the right tools. They knew that, tomorrow, they had to have every-thing they needed so they could finish the project.

As they got all the materials together, Tiny said, "Grandpa, do you think Grandma is happy?"

Tim, caught off guard, took a deep breath, thought for a sec-ond, and said, "I suppose so? But I think she misses us."

Tim and Tiny didn't speak any more of the subject and gath-ered all their needs for tomorrow's project. Once they had them all situated the way they wanted, they went inside for a manly bonding moment of a game of War while watching cartoons.

With the night nearing a late hour, Tim and Tiny washed up, changed into their PJs (matching red flannels that Grandma had got-ten them), and headed off to bed. Tiny went to his room and knelt beside his bed to say his prayers. Tim stood back silently as he lis-tened to Tiny thank God for this day, for his grandpa, for the fun, for Frankies, for his mom and dad. Then Tiny took a breath and asked God to let his grandma know that "we miss her too."

Tiny then climbed into his bed. Tim, after wiping the tears away, leaned over, kissed him on the forehead, and tucked him in. "I love you, buddy."

"I love you too…turd." They both smiled, and Tim left.

Tim sat on the edge of his bed replaying the prayer that he had just listened too. As he reflected on today's events, he realized that he had not prayed since Mary died. He yelled. He cried. He screamed. He sulked. He remembered, but he hadn't prayed. As a matter of fact, he could not remember the last time that he prayed. With a shrug of the shoulder, Tim thanked God for Tiny and the day.

Tim and Tiny rose early in the morning, got their cereal and coffee, and ate some donuts and some gummies. They made sure to take their vitamins to keep them strong, and out the shop they went to get started on their project.

First, they needed to sand each piece of wood so that it was smooth. They did not want the birds to get a splinter. As they were sanding the wood, they would tell silly stories about each piece, where it came from, and why the tree really did not want to be a tree anymore. They talked about importance of taking their time and getting all the rough edges off.

During this process, Tim took the opportunity to talk to Tiny as a man. It came to Tim that he should talk to the young man about different things he would encounter and that he would have to sand the rough edges off.

"Kiddo, can we talk?"

"I thought we were, Grandpa?"

"Yes, we are. But I was wondering if we could have a man to man talk?"

"Sure, what do you need to know?" Tiny said with a devilish grin. "Do you need me to tell you about girls? I can tell you about girls. You need me to tell you about cars? I can tell you about cars." Tiny giggled.

"Well…" Tim started.

"Well, Grandpa, girls have cooties and are annoying, but cars are cool!" Tiny interrupted.

"So correct you are, young man," Tim said with a giggling grin. "But I wanted to tell you something about this birdhouse and how it is like everything you do in life. Can we talk about that?"

Tiny stopped for a minute and looked at his grandpa with a puzzled look. His eyes were ever curious as to what on earth his grandpa was talking about. Tim continued to sand methodically, awaiting the boy's response. After a few moments, Tiny said, "Okay, Grandpa, what does building a birdhouse have to do with school or playing in the backyard?"

Without hesitation and continuing to sand carefully, Tim answered, "So you see how when we started, all the pieces were scattered all over the shop, and we had to locate everything we needed so it was easier?"

"Yes."

"Well, it is the same way in life. Everything we do is much easier when we are organized and get everything together in one place. It makes it easier to find stuff we really need or want."

"Oh…that makes sense. But, Grandpa…does that mean I need to clean my room? I don't like cleaning my room. That's boring."

With a smile on his face, Tim answered, "Yes, you should clean your room. That way, when you want your spaceman, you know where it is. Or if you need your favorite boots, you can find both of them easily. Think of cleaning your room like the walk we took in the woods. You don't want it to smell like a turd, do you?" Tim stopped sanding and winked at Tiny.

"OH, GRANDPA!" And they both began laughing.

"So you see how we are sanding off all the rough spots and edges to make the pieces smooth? Well, you are going to have rough spots that you will need to sand off the rough edges for. Like you see someone not being nice, you should go over and stand up for the person they are being mean to."

"What if they are bigger than me?"

"That is when it is the hardest, kiddo. But if you know what you are doing is right, then it is something you have to do as a man. Sometimes sanding wood, you get a splinter and it hurts. Sometimes standing up to a bully, you get a black eye and it hurts, but…in the end, the birdhouse will look wonderful, and the person you stood up for will be very thankful."

The boys finished their sanding, and the construction phase began. Tiny got the glue and carefully placed a long bead along the edge of the wood, then another, then another, and another until there was a bead on all four sides. Then carefully, they placed each wall on the glue, and Tim adjusted the wood clamps accordingly. They knew they needed to leave it alone for a couple of hours to dry, so they decided it would be a good time for a short walk in the woods.

Grabbing their jackets, they headed out for a walk in the woods. Today's adventure was a bit slower than yesterday's. Tiny was not as rambunctious as he was yesterday. While walking quietly, Tiny pointed out several woodland creatures that were scurrying around for food. Above them, he caught a squirrel jumping from one tree to another. Birds were singing, and you could hear a little more rustle in the brook waters in the distance.

"Buddy, what can you learn from that squirrel that jumped from one tree to the other?"

"That he is nuts!" he said with a hearty chuckle.

Smiling largely, Tim replied, "Okay? But what else?"

They walked along in silence for a while. Tim gave Tiny a chance to ponder the question and figure out the answer in his own way. The boys made it all the way to the brook and were watching the waters bash against the rocks and banks from the mild wind. There was a chipmunk on the other side of the brook trying to navigate a way across from where he was standing. The bridge was only thirty feet to the chipmunk's right, but he was steadfast in seeking a direct route across the water.

After about fifteen minutes of watching the chipmunk, Tiny asked Tim, "Grandpa, why doesn't he just go over there to the bridge?"

"Well, kiddo, he doesn't see it. All he sees is the water in front of him, and he knows he must get across. He is blinded to anything around him except the problem in front of him. If you watch how he is acting, it looks like he is getting nervous because he cannot figure the problem out."

"Do you think he will let me help him?"

"No, son. As soon as you go close to him, he will run off afraid of you. He does not understand that you are just trying to help him."

A few more minutes passed, and Tim reminded Tiny that they needed to start heading back. Tiny was concerned about the chipmunk, but Tim reassured him that the animal would eventually figure something out. They had almost made it back to the shop when Tiny said, "Grandpa, the squirrel. He wasn't afraid to jump because he could see where he wanted to land. And he knew he could do it. But the chipmunk was very scared even though he could see where he was wanting to go."

"That's right."

"I think I want to be like the squirrel and be not afraid to take chances. Hey...do you think the birdhouse is ready for the rest of the pieces?"

"Yes, sir, I believe it is ready. And I am glad you want to be the squirrel."

The boys went into the shop to check the project. It was ready for the roof and floor. They carefully placed glue beads on the wood and assembled the rest of the house. Tim readjusted the wood clamps to hold them in place, and now it was time for lunch.

While Tim made their sandwiches for lunch, Tiny ran to his room to get his bag. Not really sure what was in the bag, Tim asked if Tiny had brought the cat turd from the treasure hunt in the sandbox. Laughing, Tiny assured him he did not bring it. He left it in his sister's room on her pillow. Tim chuckled as the two sat down at the table to eat.

Tiny had taken a couple of hearty bites and then reached into his pockets for the items he wanted to share with his grandpa. The first thing he pulled out was an army guy with a rifle in the prone position. Tiny explained to Tim the importance of laying down to shoot a gun and that it was easier to hide if you were lying down. The next item he pulled out was a matchbox car. The car was a cool Shelby SS, jet black with flames. Tiny explained that this was his favorite car ever since he was born, that one day, when he was bigger, he was going to get one just like this one. The third thing he pulled out was a key on a chain. Puzzled, Tim asked him what the key was for. Tiny took another bite of his lunch and sat silent for moment. Then he said, "Grandpa, Grandma gave me this key. Do you know what it unlocks?"

Tim took the key and studied over it. The key looked familiar, but he was not sure what it went into. After a few moments, Tim answered, "Kiddo, I am not sure, but I have a couple of ideas. Let's finish our lunch, and we will go check it out, okay?"

"Okay."

They finished their lunch talking about the two walks in the woods, the story of the turds, the birdhouse in the shop, and the fun time they have had in just two days. Tiny asked what time he had to go home, and Tim said around dinner time. With a sad face, Tiny agreed but said, "Grandpa, I love you. I like it here." With a tear in his eye, Tim told him that he loved him and that he was glad he liked it here.

Tim took Tiny, and they went to the attic. Up there, there were three different boxes with locks on them. Those boxes were Mary's, and Tim had never paid any attention to them after she had him tote them all the way to the attic. They were heavy, and he was afraid if he showed interest, she would have him move them again…so he just did as he was asked and then forgot them…quickly.

They tried the key in each of the locks, but none of them opened. Disheartened, Tiny shrugged his shoulders and said it must be junk. Tim wrapped him up in his arms and told him that his grandma never gave away junk, that she must have given him the key to a treasure chest and that they had to find the map.

"Really?"

"Of course. Now, let's go check our birdhouse and see how it is doing."

Out the door and down the stairs Tiny ran while Tim tried to figure out where this key went and where on earth Mary put it. Did she leave a treasure map for Tiny knowing that he loved pirates? Was this something they were going to do together and, thanks to the drunk driver, now they wouldn't get to? Tim's emotions were starting to well up, and he knew he had to slow them down so as not to scare Tiny.

"Grandpaaaa…you comin'?"

"On my way."

In the shop, they noticed that the roof and walls were not setting as fast as the walls did and that they might have to wait to finish the project. They discussed possibly painting it or just leaving it or maybe staining it. Tiny wasn't sure what he wanted to do yet, but he started talking about how many birds were going to enjoy going in and out of this house. He spun the home around gently and looked at Tim with deep concern.

"Grandpa, there is no hole for them to get in."

In their storytelling and haste, Tim forgot to drill the hole for the birds to come and go in and out of. They had built a very safe birdhouse—no one in and no one out.

"Well, booger. What do you think we should do?" asked Tim

"The birds must get in… We have to make the hole. But if we make the hole now, the house might fall apart… Do we need to take it apart and start over, ya think?"

"What if you hold the house with the clamps and I very slowly drill out the hole?"

"BUT IT WILL BREAK. Won't it?"

"I am not sure, buddy, but it is worth a shot to try, don't you think?"

Tiny was scared. He and Tim had worked extremely hard on this project, and he did not want to break it. "But what if it falls apart?"

"Tiny…do you remember the squirrel and the chipmunk?"

Puzzled, Tiny nodded his head.

"Why don't we be the squirrel?"

"Okay, Grandpa. We can be the squirrel. We know where we are going, and we are not afraid!"

"That's my boy…I mean, young man."

Carefully, Tim placed Tiny's hands on the clamps for him to hold the house in place. Tim got the drill and the appropriate attachment and told Tiny that, on the count of three, he would begin to slowly drill the hole.

One.

Two.

Three.

Tim began to drill, and Tiny held on to the clamps just like he was told. Pretty soon, the hole was made, and the house was still all in one piece. Tiny's face lit up like a Christmas tree, and Tim was relieved that it worked. They cleaned up the shop and talked about a little bit of everything and planned when Tiny could come back and finish the house. Tim said the following weekend was okay with him if his mom was okay with him coming back.

The shop was cleaned up, the birdhouse was on the shelf to finish drying, and they had time for one more walk before it was time to go home.

"Where do you want to walk this time?"

"Grandpa, do we have to go for a walk?"

Perplexed, Tim replied, "No, son. What do you want to do?"

"Can we just go inside and watch cartoons together? I would really like to sit on your lap and watch cartoons."

"Absolutely, sport. Let's go in and see what we can find."

It had been a very long time, it felt like anyway, since Tiny wanted to sit on his lap for any time longer than a few seconds. Tim was quite content with the idea.

2

"Mooom, I am home!"

"Why, yes you are, young man. Did you have a good time?"

"Duh, Mom."

"Tiim," came from the back room.

"Oops, gotta run, Grandpa. Love you."

Tim laughed and watched as Tiny took off out the back door with his sister in hot pursuit.

"I take it she found the surprise he left her?"

"How did you ever guess?"

The two laughed and headed towards the kitchen. Janey asked if he would like a cup of coffee or to stay for dinner. It was pizza night, and Jack had stopped at their favorite pizza pub for one of their monster pizza pies. There would be plenty. Tim politely declined and explained that her mother had left Tiny a key, and now, Tim was on a mission to find where that key went before next weekend. He asked if it would be all right if he came and got Tiny next weekend. Janey giggled and said she needed to see if Jack made plans for the family. They had been planning an outing before it got too cold, but she would let him know.

Tim passed Jack on the way out of the city. As he drove towards the house, his mind began to wander. He was remembering all the different places he and Mary had gone. All the possibilities there could be for that key. This was his new mission in life. Find that lock, and hopefully…before next weekend.

The sun was setting, and the glorious artwork was breathtaking. Tim thought about Tiny's question about if Mary was happy and if she was with God. Transfixed and deep in thought, Tim missed his turn and was heading the wrong way. The sun set completely, and the darkness was filling the sky. By the time he recovered from his trance of thought, Tim was in an area he was not familiar with. He presumed that he had not turned but was not sure. The surroundings were not familiar. The daylight was almost gone, so that was not helping. He had left his phone at home because he was tired of being tethered. After all, he had lived a great many years without a phone…why should he carry one all the time now?

Tim got his truck turned around and started back the way he had come to the best of his knowledge. He was not too keen on having to drive in an area foreign to him. He still had half a tank of gas, so he was not too concerned but did not want to think about having to walk out of this area without realizing where he was. Though the area where they moved was safe, he was not sure how close to his home he was and if this area was safe.

Focused on the road, Tim thought of how he and Tiny had made the doorway for the birds. They trusted they would land where they needed to safely. Tim told himself that he was the squirrel and would land safely. Lost in that thought, he passed his turn again, and the next thing he saw was the lights of the city where Janey and Jack lived. He decided he would pop in and see if they could spot him a place to sleep; he obviously did not need to be driving tonight.

When Tim explained to them what happened, they all laughed and said there was a fold-up bed he could sleep on. Tiny and his sister rolled it out of the closet and commenced to getting it ready for Grandpa. This was a grand time for the two of them; they had never had a sleepover of this caliber before.

While the kids made up Tim's bed, Janey made him a plate of monster pizza and grabbed him a Coke. They sat around the table and talked and listened to the war going on down the hall in making the bed. Laughter rang out as Tim started to tell stories about Janey and some of her antics as a child.

The kids finally finished making up the bed and were proud of the accomplishment. Janey asked which room they put the bed in. Both kids looked at each other and then their mother and said, "Room?"

All three adults got up and looked down the hallway; the bed had been parked in the widest part of the hallway and made up for Tim to sleep in. No one could get to the bathroom or the office, but the guest bed was finished. With gut-wrenching laughter, the three went down and maneuvered the bed into Tiny's room. Tiny thought that was the coolest.

The night pressed on, and the family enjoyed a video chat with the other families so that Tim could tell of his senior moment all at once. They discussed the upcoming holidays, the when and the where. Each child offered to host if Tim was not comfortable with hosting. Tim thanked them each but said that Mary would have wanted the tradition to continue as it had been, and he would do his best to make it the same. He did make the request that they bring some food, because his cooking was no way near as good as his Mary's. They all agreed on who would bring what, and both Thanksgiving and Christmas were scheduled. They came to a close, and the chat ended. By now, the little ones were curled up on the couch asleep. Jack picked up Maggie, and Tim picked up Tiny. Tim gave Janey a peck on the cheek and headed off to bed.

3

Walking through the woods, Tim noticed the scenery was off. It was like he had not ever been here before. The underbrush was full of thick thorny thickets, and trees were in full bloom, but they should be near barren. He noticed that he had a sickle to cut through the thickets but was not sure how to use it properly. Tim was swinging and slashing, but the thicket thorns seemed to be alive and striking back. Tim found himself in the middle of his woods that did not seem to be his woods and stuck without a solid or simple way out. He could hear moaning in the distance but could not lay eyes on anything or anyone. He called out, but there was no answer. Feverishly, he swung the sickle to break a path for him to get through, but nothing seemed to be working. Getting more and more frustrated, Tim could hear a voice.

"Grandpa…Grandpa…"

Tim started fighting the thickets and vines. He had to get to Tiny. He didn't know where he was or if he was in trouble, and not being able to see or move caused Tim to panic.

"Dad…Dad…DAD!" Janey shouted.

*****

Tim woke from his dream. "Wha…what? What is going on?"

"Dad, you were flinging your arms back and forth like you were fighting a bear."

"Did you win, Grandpa?" asked Tiny

"Did I win?"

"Yeah, did you win against the bear Mom said you were fighting?"

"Oh, I don't know, kiddo. It was a weird dream for sure. What time is it?"

"It is 7:00 a.m. I am making coffee. Would you like a pot for yourself?" Janey said with a smirk.

"Yes…at least one pot."

Tim arrived home shortly after 11:00 a.m. The mail was in the box, and he made his way up to the house. As he flipped through the pieces of mail, he began to think about the dream he had at Janey's and what it could possibly mean. He was not a fan of a puzzle like this. He liked order and understanding.

He grabbed himself a glass and filled it with ice water and then went into the office and sat down behind the computer. It wasn't on, and he was not a big gizmo geek. He knew how to use it; he just chose not to.

He looked around the room at all the pictures, books, mementos, and memories Mary had put in this room. She would spend hours playing a game or shopping when the weather was not nice for her to be outside. In the corner above the bookshelf, he spotted a cobweb and chuckled. He looked at the books on the shelf and remembered each one she got and how she proclaimed this one would be different and she would finish it. Tim did not think she ever finished one of them. That, in itself, made him chuckle too. On the wall, just under the cobweb, was a picture of when they went on vacation. There was no plan. There was no route. There was no time frame. It was just the two of them, in the car, on the road, with nowhere to be. They took a week to run away and found out at the end that they had only gone about sixteen hours away, straight trip, from their home. But that was okay. Where they took this picture, they met some of the nicest people. To the right of the picture, on a shelf, he noticed another treasure. It was a photo of his dad and mom on the day he got back from the war. She had met him at the airport.

Tim began to weep. All this time, he had turned a cold shoulder to his mom's death and focused on his loss of Mary. What of the companionship he had had with his mother? Why did her death not affect him the way Mary's did? For goodness' sake, she gave birth to him. Why is he being so cold?

The day drudged on, and Tim sank lower and lower in thought about why he was not mourning over the loss of his mother like he was the loss of his wife. Why did her death not seem to matter as much as Mary's? How could he be so callous? What an awful son he was.

Tim walked throughout the house apologizing to his mother for not being a better son. For not being able to protect her like she had protected him. Sorry for not mourning for her like a true son would mourn. Then, when all his apologies were done, he got mad because now he was a crazy old man talking to himself in an empty house to a dead woman. What was his problem?

Before heading to bed, he decided to go back into the office. Something was telling him that he needed to go back in. He walked in and turned on the light. When the light came on, something sparkled out of the corner of his right eye. He jolted his head to catch whatever it was, but nothing jumped out at him. Staring deeply in the area he saw the sparkle, he shut the light off, let his eyes adjust to the dark, and *then* flipped on the light. Nothing. Now he was annoyed because he knew he saw something. He walked over to where he thought it might be and moved things around, but nothing sparkled. He was not a happy camper, and now, adding to his moment of crazy talk in his front room, now he was seeing things. Great…this was how his life was going to be…*nuts*.

Tim took himself to bed. He sat on the edge and thought about Tiny's prayer the other night. As he sat there, he heard a distant voice saying that Tiny was just a kid and that was what kids did. *You don't need to worry about that. You are a grown man. You can take care of yourself. Besides, why would he listen to you? You don't even care that your mother died with your wife. You are horrible.* Downtrodden, Tim laid down and went to sleep.

The next morning, Tim woke up with a headache. He did not sleep well and felt like he had tossed and turned all night long. He truly felt like he had wrestled a bear and lost. He found and took the headache medicine Mary had bought. It was good stuff. Usually, within a few minutes, you would feel ten times better. Tim made himself a cup of coffee and some toast. He went outside to watch the sun come up. As he sat there in the dark with his coffee, he started to reminisce about the dream and the thoughts he had been having. None of it was making any sense to him, and as far as he could tell, they were the cause of his headache. Whenever Tim would get a puzzle he could not solve, he would work himself into such a tizzy that his head would feel like it was about to explode. This was one of those times. Nothing was making any sense, and he was annoyed.

Sitting there, he could hear a barn owl on the other side of the brook. Some kind of animal was rummaging around the shop. The brook was silent this morning. There was a gentle breeze, but not too cold. He finished his toast and coffee and thought he had done that awfully fast because there was no sign of the sun. And usually, by the time he finished his coffee and toast, the sun would be breaking the crest of the horizon. He got up and decided that maybe he just needed another cup, but as he walked in the house, he noticed that the clock said it was only 3:00 a.m. *Good grief,* he thought, *no wonder I am tired. I am going back to bed.*

*****

Tim was standing on the bridge at the brook. The chipmunk that he and Tiny had seen three days ago was still standing in the same place, trying to get across the now still water. The look of extreme fright was infused on his face. Tim decided to approach carefully to see if he could help the little guy out. Just as Tim got to him and reached down to pick him up, the little guy bolted forward without a worry and cleared the brook in one leap. Tim was amazed that the little guy could jump so far without a running start. Perhaps his adrenaline was pumped so high that it was all he needed—the fear of Tim helping him.

Night fell quickly, and the woods went completely dark. Tim did not bring a light of any kind, and now, had to figure out how to get back to his house. Using what little bit of moonlight that had trickled into the area where he was, Tim managed to get back to the bridge and across to his side. First hurdle down. *Now there is just that mile trek back to the house with nothing to guide me. This ought to be blast.* Tim was thinking that if he was not careful, he could easily find himself on the other side of the woods completely bypassing his house without even realizing it. With each step, he attempted to focus his eyesight on glimmers of moonlight in hopes that familiar landmarks would guide him to the house and not the other side of the property.

Tim knew it was roughly a mile. He knew that, in daylight, it would take him about thirty minutes to navigate back, partly because he was getting older and his legs tended to give way on this uneven ground. So he figured an hour in the pitch of night should be sufficient to get back to the house. He looked down at his watch to note the time so he would know how bad off he was.

Each step was carefully placed in front of or beside the other. Trickles of moonlight guided his path. He could hear the neighbor's barn owl getting further away. He felt like that was a good sign.

Splash. Splash.

What on Earth was that? Tim looked down, and he was standing in the brook. Totally confused because he had left the brook when it got dark, Tim was now standing knee-deep in the brook. That was not possible. *How did I end up back here?* he thought.

4

Bang, bang, bang, bang, bang, bang, bang, bang, bang.

Startled, Tim jolted, and he was awake. Confused and bewildered, he looked at his watch and it was now 8:00 a.m. Exhausted, he got up from his bed and headed to the sounds of the banging. It was the trash truck. The worker was using the lift to beat the trash can and empty it into the truck. Tim wiped his eyes and headed for the kitchen. The coffee was still hot, so he got himself a new cup and sat down at the table. He could hear the trash truck driving away as he thought to himself, *Why am I having these weird dreams? The dreams wear me out more than actual work.*

Tim finished his coffee and thought he might go see if he could find the treasure that Mary had left for Tiny. She had not mentioned it to him, so when Tiny showed him the key, he was caught off guard. He went back into the office, and something sparkled as he entered. Carefully, he walked over to the area that caught his eye. Then the sparkle lit once again. It was the reflection of the glass covering the picture on top of the desk. It was a picture he did not ever remember seeing. It was a picture of her and Tiny down at the brook, and in the picture, she was wearing a chain with a key on it. In the picture, both were smiling at each other, and on the bottom, it had written on it, "Jeremiah 29:11."

He placed the picture down and looked around the room to see if there was a box or something that the key Tiny had would fit and open. Nothing. Shrugging his shoulders, he decided to search the closet in their bedroom. She still had lots of stuff she had not gotten around organizing. Maybe the container was in there.

As he opened her closet, her scent overwhelmed him. The scent of his soul mate, his love, his heart, came permeating out when he opened the door. A wave of emotion hit him hard. He sank to the floor and began to weep. Why did she have to die? Why was that driver even on the road? Why did his mom have to be with her? How was he supposed to be strong when he felt so weak? How was he supposed to live without the love of his life or the guidance of his matriarch? Why did they both have to go? Why not just one, then he would at least still have one of his supports here with him?

Which one would you choose?

"Huh?"

Which one would you choose?

Which one would you choose to die?

"Who said that? Who's here?" Tim looked up to see that the room was empty. But he had heard clearly a quiet voice ask him, scheming-like, who would he choose to die? What kind of morbid nonsense was that?

Fighting the tears and flood of emotions, Tim carefully went through each box in the bottom of the closet. None of them had a lock of any sort. He ran across a series of boxes that contained pictures. Lots and lots of pictures. Here was one from when they took Jon camping for the first time. Boy, he did not like the dirt. Here was one of Maggie when she was born. What a doll. Here was the last Christmas before Dad passed away. Here was one of when they first bought the house. And another of Tiny and Mary. She had that key on there too. Hmmm. Interesting. There was a shadow behind her, but the sun was going down behind her, so how was there a shadow? Weird.

Tim laid the pictures off to the side. He wanted to look at them more closely later. Through all the boxes, he found birth photos, Jack and Janey's wedding, Jon's graduation, old military pictures, and the list of memories went on. Tim decided that he wanted to organize the treasure trove of pictures. Now he had to come up with a plan on how he wanted them separated. Would it be by year (ish) or by kid (ish).

He went to the office and got a marker, a pad of paper, and some items to use as paperweights. He decided he would separate by person, and then he would attempt to organize by year. He emptied the first four small containers in an attempt to make his base. Then he moved to a larger container. The piles were starting to blend, so he used the empty containers to reorganize. That also helped with keeping them separated. As he came to the last container of pictures, he had several memory mountains going on.

In order to keep some kind of orderly fashion in place, he carefully lifted himself off the floor and then resituated himself so he could more easily maneuver around and then neatly disseminate the pictures accordingly. By the end of the filing and restacking, Tim had managed to create twenty-five separate piles of people, places, and things that they had pictures of. Fifteen of those piles had their own containers, but he was going to have to manufacture containers for the other ten piles. Tim went on a scavenger hunt for boxes and empty containers. In just a short amount of time, he was able to conjure up enough containers to help keep himself organized. Feeling accomplished, Tim decided it was time get outside for some fresh air. As he passed the clock in the kitchen, he noticed it was mid-afternoon. "Good thing I didn't have anything to do today," he chuckled.

Out to the shop he went and checked on the setting of the birdhouse. It was holding nicely. Before releasing the clamps, he decided it would be better to sand the entry point from the fresh cut. That way, it would have more stability while he was sanding.

Admiring his and Tiny's work, Tim heard a voice.

So…nice birdhouse you have there. You and your grandson did a great job. Wonder if your wife would have liked it?

Tim paused in his sanding and thought, *Wonder if Mary would have liked this. Duh, of course she would. She liked everything I have made.*

Did you know that she did not like the table you made? She only said she did because you kept going on about it. She did not want to hurt your feelings. She told her friend Ethel that it was "goofy" the way you did it. If she truly liked it, she would not have said that.

He began to think of the table he had made for her. *She cooed and aww-ed over it like it was big diamond ring. She really did like it. But why would she say it was goofy. Ha! Well, dummy, you did make the legs all different sized and had to adjust. Of course it was goofy.* Tim laughed and continued to sand.

Did you know she had a secret love? His name was Tim also.

What? Huh? Who is in here? Tim looked around, and there was no one in the room. *Why am I thinking like this? This is crazy.*

Tim completed the sanding and removed the clamps. The birdhouse was finished. Now he just needed to weatherize it so it could sit outside. Should he wait for Tiny or just go ahead? *The house is not hurting anything sitting here. I will wait until I get to talk to him again. After all, it is not my project, but our project.*

Over the course of the next few days, Tim went about his normal activities—coffee, toast, relaxing; you know, the normal stuff for a retiree. But Thursday had rolled around, and he remembered that he had to check with Janey about Tiny coming over.

As the phone rang, it came to mind that he still had not figured out the key thing. What could it possibly go into?

"Hello?"

"Hello, my dear. How are you doing this fine and dandy day?"

"Dad? Are you okay?"

"Well, of course, why do you ask?"

"Well, to start with, you never sound like Mary Poppins. It is always Eeyore," she said with a chuckle.

"Ha-ha, very funny," he replied. "So I am calling about this weekend. Can I come get Tiny? Or did Jack make family plans?"

"Sorry, Dad. I meant to call you earlier in the week to let you know. Jack did get the weekend off, so we are taking the kids camping one last time before it gets too cold. You can come too if you want."

"Hmm, sleep on the ground or a rock-hard cot in the colder temperatures...or...sleep in my climate-controlled soft and cozy bed? Let me see. Welp...the cramp in my knee at that thought says I think I will pass," Tim answered with a hearty chuckle.

The two spoke for the next hour or so on where they were going, whatever Tim would do with Tiny to keep him in line, and what each of them were going to have for dinner. Tim explained that he would be continuing to look for the container that the key that Tiny had would fit into. He explained that he had gone through some pictures and found a couple with Mary wearing that same key. Janey told him that she was not aware of any key, that it must be a secret between Tiny and the grandparents. "Ya know, parents are not in the cool club like grandparents."

Tim laughed and wished them a good, fun, and safe outing and said he would be thinking of them while he curled up in his bed at night. After the conversation concluded, Tim went back to the office. Something kept nagging at him that what he wanted was in there... somewhere. But where?

Standing in the doorway, Tim gazed about the room, and that one lonely cobweb caught his eye. With a giggle, he decided that it would be a good idea to clean and organize this room so that he would have a place for his and Tiny's organization of the family photo project. Plus, with any kind of luck, he would find the container that the key opened. After all, this was primarily Mary's room. If it would be anywhere, it would make sense that it would be in here.

The first thing to do would be to relocate the items off the shelving unit and neatly stack them in the front room (out of the way, of course). Then remove the shelving unit and dust it off. Tim had decided that he would systematically clean the room. He would start on one side and move his way around. As he moved and or dusted items, he would wipe down the wall around it to make sure that Mr. Cobweb was homeless. He figured that if he was going to clean the room, he might as well be thorough, because it would probably be a very long time before he had the desire to do it again.

There were quite a lot of trinkets and books on the shelving unit. More than he had anticipated, even though he was looking at them. They seemed to multiply with each one he removed. Almost like a dark void of everything and nothing. With each item though, he would recall certain memories and enjoy the moment. Once he finished the shelving unit, he moved it to just the hallway. He did not see the point in really exercising and moving it to the front room only to move it back. However, after getting it moved to the hallway, he really did not move it back far enough, and now he was stuck in the room. That would not have been so bad except the cleaning supplies were in the front room. He did not think this through.

Standing in the doorway, wishing he had done better losing weight, he contemplated moving the unit back in, going to get the supplies, and then moving it back out so that he could move it back in after he was done. That was a whole lot of moving, and that was not in the cards. So he decided it would be better to climb out the window, walk around, get the supplies and then climb back in the window. That would be the smarter thing to do.

As he was getting ready to climb out of the window, he could see Mary in his mind shaking her head and asking him just what in tarnation he thought he was doing. Laughing loudly, he audibly replied, "Doing it my way," and promptly lost his balance, falling out of the window with a mighty *thud!*

Once Tim had finished that wall and put everything back in its place, he set out to do the next wall. Methodically, he pulled items off shelves and placed them in the front room, moved shelves—this time within the room—and cleaned the wall behind them, and washed the shelves and then replaced the items he had moved off. As he worked his way around the room, he thought to himself, *I wonder if Mary has passed out yet.* When he approached the desk, he thought to himself, *How am I going to tackle this?* With a hearty sigh, he audibly shouted, "My way, of course!" and laughed. He could see Mary beside herself wanting to tell him that if he broke her stuff, she would take him out.

As he was moving stuff about the desk, he found another photo with Mary and that necklace with a key. He found it odd that he had never (1) seen her wear that key, (2) even knew about that key, or (3) seen these pictures before. Where were they taken?

Did you know she had a secret life? Did you know that there was another man? She loved him more than you. That key is his. To his place. Did you know that?

"*Huh!* Wait! What! Who said that?" Quickly, Tim realized that it was that weird voice he kept hearing. He didn't know who or why because there was no one there but him and his imagination.

Tim finished the room, shaking off this weird voice. He knew that Mary was faithful. He knew she didn't have another man in her life. He was not even sure where that nonsense thought came from.

Why would he even consider that she had another man? That was completely ridiculous.

While cleaning the desk cubbies and drawers, Tim ran across ticket stubs for a concert that they had attended many years ago. Thinking, *Why would she still have those?* he remembered that night. It was an open-air concert. The day had started out a bit balmy, but by mid-evening, it was like someone turned on the freezer controls and it was cold. They hadn't really planned for this kind of climate change; they had planned for rain, not arctic freeze. They did not want to leave the concert, so they maneuvered their way into the middle of the crowd—for the warmth, of course—and then pretended to be much younger. They jumped up and down and danced with the crowd as if they were teenagers. And the crowd they were in, though not teens, were *much* younger than they were. By the end of the concert, they were the coolest old people and the sorest. What a night that was.

Carefully, Tim rummaged through the desk and found treasure trove after treasure trove. Each memory brought back warmth and a lot of stories that he really should share with the kids and grandkids. They needed to know what kind of grandma Mary really was when she wasn't feeding them.

In the top middle drawer, there was a Bible. It was Mary's mothers. She had gotten it at the funeral after all was done. Her siblings were not believers and did not care what happened to it. Mary wanted to have the long-lasting memory of her mom. Also, in there was her family tree. Her mom had been working the family heritage when she got sick. Annabelle worked on it almost to the day that she died. Mary had tried to keep up with it, but with all the other gazillion projects she had, it just kind of fell by the wayside.

Tim started flipping through the book and was reading the comments in the margins and then the verses they were next to. He laughed and said, "This was probably aimed at Dick and this one at Tina." He laughed at how vocal Annabelle had been in her Bible. He had not seen anyone "write" in a Bible. He always thought it was against the rules. But he found that this was the best reading he had ever run across and decided to sit for a spell and enjoy the movie.

He could see Annabelle as plain as day and her temperament as she scribed these quick notes. He could also envision her saying these things.

He was about a good twenty or thirty pages into the notations when it dawned on him that no one seemed to be left out of her sights…but him. There were no comments of him. In the pages that he had read, she seemed to have tagged everyone in the family, including Mary and her siblings, but he was not mentioned. This perplexed him as to when she wrote these things and if they were written before he and Mary got together. It was another puzzle for him to figure out. *But then*, he thought, *maybe I was the good one and she left me alone, or maybe she had it out of her system by the time Tim came along.*

Tim read another thirty or so pages before he decided that he better get off his duff and finish this room. *I have been at this all day and am almost finished.* Tim took the Bible into the bedroom and put it on his nightstand. He figured he could read more of Annabelle's antics when he needed a good read.

The next item he found of interest was a folded-up paper that seemed like a treasure map. He was ecstatic. *This must have something to do with the key. I have it, and I will put it in with the Bible, and when I go get Tiny, we can figure it out together. Ha! I knew it was in here.*

Very pleased with himself, Tim promptly and diligently finished off Mary's room in high fashion. Everything was dusted, washed, and organized. He even got the little closet organized. He found some more pictures to go through and separate, and he found another Bible that he had not seen before. He just put it in the other room with Annabelle's and figured he would find some more notes to laugh at.

As he finished the room, he admired his handiwork. He thought about the adventure it had been to just do this one room and was thinking that he needed to be a bit more organized for the next room he decided to tackle. Fortunately, it looked like this was the last room Mary had not gotten to, so until he was ready to change things, he was quite content with the way the rest of the house was.

5

Thanksgiving was closing in. It was just in two weeks. Tim and Tiny had finished the birdhouse, and it had been placed out the back door near the porch. The key was still a mystery. The treasure map was one that Tiny had drawn for Mary one day while she was watching him. Tiny remembered it because it was just before she died. The house was cleaned and organized, and Tim felt that even Mary would approve. He had even been to some open markets to purchase gourds and other décor for the festivities. He had found all the Christmas stuff too and placed it in one of the bedrooms so that, maybe after celebrating Thanksgiving, he and the family could decorate the tree and the house. He thought that Mary would appreciate that.

Tiny was supposed to come over on the weekend, and they were going to see what kind of trouble they could get into. The picture project was kind of on the back burner because every time Tim opened a new door, he would find what he felt was a ton of pictures. He finally had to move the containers out of his room and into the office but carefully organized so they could be gotten to easily. He had run across several more pictures of Mary and that key, but he still had no recollection of it or the photos that he found. He was reading out of Annabelle's margins a few pages every night, and where she did not specify a name, he imagined who she was speaking of. Occasionally, he would find himself reading the scriptures and wondering what they meant.

Night was falling, and he was about done for. He had worked outside all day raking, trimming, and cleaning up the yard. He wanted to have most of this work done before Tiny got there because he wanted to focus on fun and adventure while he was there.

Tim went in and plopped into his chair. He was hungry, but not enough to get up and fix himself something. He leaned down to take off his boots and heard his back crack. Tim thought, *Oh no, that felt good, but am I going to be able to move?* He figured, while he was down there, that he would finish removing his shoes. At least he would have that done. Slowly and carefully, he sat back up in his chair, and with a mighty "whew," he said, "Now that feels a lot better."

She had another man in her life. You are stupid to think that she didn't. Your job kept you away until you retired, and even after you retired, you did what you wanted. You never really did help out around here. She started looking at this other guy right after Annabelle died. He is tall, dark, handsome, and she fell head over heels in love with him. She would go see him every weekend. Sometimes she would squeeze in time in the middle of the week. That key is to his house. You are a fool to think that she really loved "just" you. This other man stole her heart and her mind. She would talk to him several times throughout the day. She would even tell him intimate things about you. He would talk to her through letters, stories, and poetry. He would speak of ancient times of history, and she was mesmerized by his voice. He would use a soothing soft voice, and she would fall into his arms. You never had a chance once he came into her life. They have had a secret affair for two years. What a fool you are."

"What? Huh? This makes no sense."

Your "wife" was having an affair with another man. One much older than you. One that knew how to make her happy. You want to know the best part? Loser. Your mom, your mother, *she introduced them. Don't you think it is ironic that both your mom and your wife died at the same time? Don't you think it was convenient for them? I mean, really, if it had just been your wife and you found out, you could have confirmed it, but just by chance, they were in the same car. I wonder if they planned it that way? Maybe it wasn't an accident. Maybe they decided it was too much, and maybe they ran into the drunk, and now that poor guy is going to pay the price. I think they had a very guilty conscience and committed suicide?*

"Nooo!"

Tim woke up in a dead fast sweat, swinging at the air. Who was in the house talking all these lies? Who were they? *Where* were they? Breathing like he had just ran a marathon and his arms cramping from the air boxing, Tim looked vigilantly around and throughout the house. There was no one there.

Sweat was pouring off his forehead. His heart was racing. He needed air. Out to the back porch, he stepped in the cool of the night. The sun was just about gone over the horizon, and Tim was frantic as to why he was having these thoughts. He knew Mary was committed to him and only him. They had been married for near on thirty years. She was faithful to Tim as he was to her. They had made a promise in the beginning that if things could not be worked out, they would go their separate ways, and everything had been worked out. Why would he be having these thoughts now? Why would he want to desecrate her memory? Was he losing his mind?

The pictures with the key necklace were bothering him. Why had he never seen that chain before or any of those pictures? Who took them? It seemed that every time he opened a new drawer or cubby or box, he would find another one. Another picture of another scene that he had never been a witness to. Was this why he thought she was having an affair? Was this why that eerie voice in his head was talking like that?

6

In the silence of the night, Tim watched the moon rise and listened to the animals scurrying around the woods. He could hear the barn owl across the way and the wind gently billowing the leaves about the ground. The night air was brisk but refreshing. In the whistle of the breeze, Tim heard a voice. A barely audible voice in the distance.

"Who is there?"

There was no answer. Then he heard the same voice again but could not make out the words.

"Who is there? This is not funny. Come out where I can see you!" Tim commanded.

After the evening he had had, Tim was in no mood for someone to play a spooky prank on him. He grabbed a flashlight and bat (just in case). Tim proceeded to walk about the property to see if he could find the voice. Though he had a light and bat, he was not nervous; this voice seemed soothing, not agitating like in his dreams.

The voice whispered again, but he still could not make out the words. Now he was annoyed and decided "whatever" and went back to the house.

Thanksgiving came, and all the kids came for dinner. The spread was huge. Mary would have been proud. They sat and talked for hours about holidays past and how this year would be the start of a new tradition since Mary was gone. They spoke of the upcoming Christmas celebration they would have and how they would honor Mary. The boys all went out to the woods and found a tree while the ladies cleaned up the dinner mess. By the time the boys got back, the girls had the decorations ready to go. The men got the tree set sturdily in the stand and began to string the lights. As the family began to decorate the tree, Tiny asked Tim to step outside for a minute.

"Grandpa? Can I ask you a question?"

"Yes, sir, you sure can. Anything you want. Just ask."

"Do you believe in God?"

Puzzled at his question, Tim replied hesitantly, "Um, yeah…I guess so. Why do you ask?"

"Well," Tiny started in a soft voice. "Well, you always seem like you are faking a smile. And, well, I heard you in the barn crying and yelling at God for taking Grandma to heaven. You used bad words and said you hated Him for taking Grandma away. So I…" Tiny paused and looked Tim in the eye. "I prayed for you that night before I went to sleep. Then I heard you in your room crying and talking to God about our day together. But you …but you don't ever talk about Grandma or Granny or God or the accident. You…just seem sad."

Tim just stood there listening to this young man speak from his heart to his grandpa.

"Dad, is everything okay?" Janey stepped out the door to check on the "toddlers" as she called them. "We are ready to put the angel on the tree. This year, we want you to do it for Mom."

With tears in his eyes, Tim hugged Tiny, and they both went inside and completed the tree and had some good old-fashioned fun. As the day came to a close, Tiny's conversation resonated in Tim's head. The kids all left, each giving an extra-long and hearty hug as they departed. When it was Tiny's turn to hug Tim—he had waited to be last—Tim got down on the floor. Tiny grabbed a hold of Tim's neck and held on tight. Tim was moved at the love he could feel in that little boy. He held on tight for a very long time and whispered in Tim's ear, "This is from Grandma. She told me to give you this." Tiny released the hug and gave Tim the necklace with the key. "Grandpa, Grandma is okay. She loves you, and she misses you."

Janey was standing nearby, and the tears were flowing steadily from her cheeks. She had talked to Tiny about God and Mary and the accident a few times and if Tim believed in God. Janey knew her dad was very angry and hurt but was not sure if she really knew his beliefs. It was not like they spent every Sunday in church. They were just a normal family that did things on Sunday.

Tim stood in the doorway as the last car left the driveway. He wiped his eyes and his nose several times. He looked intently at the necklace and wondered what the key went into. Why would Tiny give up a gift that Mary had given him? Why would the boy ask about God? When did he hear him in the barn? Because the day that Tim had his screaming fit at God, he was home alone. How did he know? What was this all about? So many questions, no answers, only tears and heartache. Why did that drunk have to take his Mary? What was this constant voice that said she was having an affair? Why did he always have to look sad? He was supposed to be the strong one. He was supposed to be the leader. He was supposed to hold everyone else up. Why did he feel like such a failure? Why did God—if there was one—take his Mary? Why did the drunk live? It was not fair!

Tim poured himself a glass of brandy and sat down in his chair. He had retrieved the Bible from the nightstand. He wasn't really sure *why* he did; he assumed it had to do with Tiny's speech. He sipped a drink, opened the Bible, and started flipping through the pages. He did not know what he was looking for and was not even reading the notes in the margins anymore. He was aimlessly flipping the pages. Every so often, he would stop because he thought something caught his eye, but when he went to read, he did not know what it was he thought he saw.

Lies.

Tim sipped another drink. As he continued to flip the pages, tears fell from his eyes. He did not know why he was crying. It just felt like it was time to cry.

If you repent, I will restore you.

Lies.

If you repent, I will restore you.

Tim's gaze was affixed on this half sentence. *If you repent, I will restore you. If you repent, I will restore you. If you repent, I will restore you.* Over and over and over, Tim read these words. "If I repent, he will restore me. Does that mean he will give me my Mary back? Does that mean he will take away the pain? What does that mean?"

Crying out the words over and over loudly, he begged someone to tell him what it meant. He was alone. He had no one anymore. No one could tell him what it meant or why he was reading it.

Lies.

Why do I keep hearing voices telling me it is all lies? There is no one here. Why do I hear voices? Why!

Tim awoke the next morning still in his chair. There was half a glass of Brandy still by his side. The Bible was still open on the page with "If you repent, I will restore you." Still unclear as to what it all meant, Tim decided he would take a walk after breakfast. When he got up from his chair, he noticed that the necklace that Tiny had given him was tightly wrapped around his hand and that he was clutching it.

After breakfast and a shower, Tim prepared for a long day in the woods. He needed to get out of the house and clear his head. Only in the woods did he realize that he was at peace. He thought that he would go down to the bridge and listen to the gurgling brook and relax. He would take some coffee and snacks just in case it turned into an all-day adventure…which he was hoping for. He really needed to think.

It had been several weeks since Tim had taken a long walk in the woods by himself to relax. He had gone on several adventures with Tiny, and he had taken a few short trips looking for the noise he could hear from the back porch; however, it felt like he had not been to the woods like this for a very long time except in his dreams.

Fall had taken its toll on the trees and the underbrush. The leaves were all about the ground, and the thickets, for some weird reason, seemed to be growing. Tim thought it odd, but hey, it was a weird time for him. He made his way to the bridge and sat down. The water was moving gently, the sound was refreshing and relaxing. Tim poured himself a thermos cap of coffee and watched in mesmerized delight at the activity and lack thereof in front of him. He sat and thought about the last few months. Mary's death. Tiny's necklace. Janey's face after Tiny gave Tim the necklace. Tim realized that Janey had not been as vocal on different subjects as she normally had been. He wondered if it was because of Mary's death. He thought about how his mother was gone as well and how he did not seem to be mourning her as heavily as he was Mary. He did not understand why, but it was not a serious contention with him. He could see Mary's face in the water smiling up at him. Then the words he read last night rushed into his mind. *If you repent, I will restore you.* What did it mean? How would he be restored? It was all confusing.

Tim sat on the bridge for several hours thinking and relaxing. Most of the thermos was gone, and he had just about depleted his snacks. He was getting the nibbles and really did not want to head back to the house yet. He reached into his pack one last time to see if he had missed anything and pulled out the necklace. Puzzled, he said, "I left this on the counter. How did it get in here?"

She was having an affair. Don't forget that. That necklace was probably a gift from her lover.

"Who said that?" Tim turned around but found no one.

Grandpa, do you believe in God?

Repent and I will restore you.

My son, I am here.

Tim heard whispers, lots of whispers, but could swear that he heard, "My son, I am here." It sounded like his father who had died decades ago.

Tim searched the area for anyone who might be close by that he had just not heard because he was deep in thought, but he saw no one. He heard whispers in the distance but could not make out what they were saying. It was kind of spooky, but not at the same time. Though he could not make out what they were saying, it felt like he was relaxing with each sound. So he set his mind at ease and just listened to the whispers…as whispers. His mind began to wander back to Annabelle's Bible and the notes in the margins. He remembered one note about how two of her friends needed to go into a fire and hoped someone liked them enough to protect them because they were super haughty. In another part, there was a piece of paper that said Agnes really liked to eat for the glory…too much, in her opinion. (Agnes was a rather large woman in Annabelle's church who was always first in line in the fellowship hall—as told by Annabelle on several occasions.) Tim laughed. He thought about a comment she had made about when Jesus turned water to into wine and that if Henry had been there then, there would not have been any left for anyone else. He thought about the story he had read about a bunch of men lowering a crippled man into a room from the roof. Why would anyone do this?

The whispers continued, and Tim found himself drifting into a relaxed state—almost to the place of slumber. It was a little too cool to be out here sleeping, but he really didn't want to lose this moment. This was the most peace he had felt since even before Mary died. He thought that, surely if he fell asleep, his body would wake him before he got into any danger. He was a pretty savvy outdoorsman. The whispers of the woods put Tim to sleep.

"Repent and I will restore you." You do know that is a lie right. No one can "restore" you. All you have is yourself and your strength. Your wife was an unfaithful woman who made a fool out of you. You bought into it, and now the whole world thinks you are an idiot. You need to just go out and find someone who will appreciate you. Quit mourning over someone who obviously had an affair. Even your grandchildren know about the affair. Your grandson gave you his locket.

Be still, my son. Do not listen to the liar. I am here. I have never left you.

Really, where were you while she was having an affair? Where were you when she died? You are never there. You left him all alone.

Son, I am here. Listen to my voice. Mary loved you with all her heart and soul. She did not have the affair the liar speaks of. She was committed to you and your family. Do not listen to him.

Hahahahaha! You were who she was having an affair with, and you dare tell him differently?

Tim woke up from his nap, no longer refreshed but drained. That was the weirdest dream. It was like watching a heated debate with two people he knew but didn't know, and he didn't know who to believe. The voice of the whispers was the one she was having an affair with, but the whispers made him feel relaxed... How could that be? The other voice made him agitated and restless. He was so confused.

Be still, my son. I am here.

"Who is this?" Tim shouted.

Frustrated that a perfectly beautiful day seemed to have been for nothing because he was now all worked up again and still did not understand what was going on in his head, Tim gathered his things and began to head for the house. Maybe another hot shower would warm him up and relax him again.

Tim got back to the house, unloaded his pack, and headed for the shower. That little nap in the woods was a mistake; he was cold to the bone. But at least he was right that he would wake up before he was in danger. He turned on some gentle music, jumped into the shower, and turned it on as hot as he could stand it. As the water pelted him, he reflected on his day, and it was funny how he ignored the chaos at the end and zeroed in on the peaceful melody of the woods. Letting his mind focus on those moments, Tim could feel the tension leave his body. His mind was in a simple moment of ease. A great feeling. He was not sure why, but he did not want the moment to end.

When the hot water began to run out, Tim decided he had been cold enough for the day and ended his tranquil shower. The music was still playing in the foggy moist bathroom, and he felt great.

Lies.

"Whatever," Tim said to the little stupid voice in his head, and he continued to get ready for bed. It was not even close to bedtime yet, but why get dressed only to get undressed again? Besides, who would see him in his jammies? Comfort was the name of the game at this point.

Folding the towels neatly over the rack, Tim got his tractor pajamas on that Tiny had gotten him last Christmas. Seemed like a good time to wear them since they were flannel, and he didn't want to get cold again.

Tim sat down in his chair with Annabelle's Bible in his lap. He was starting to find it intriguing. Without even realizing it, he was reading story after story after story. He was finding it hard to settle down, though he did find himself shaking his head a lot and asking if people were truly that stupid. Like really, if someone were feeding you every day and only had one rule, why would you do something to mess that up? If someone helped you get away from those that were hurting you, why wouldn't you want to do what they asked? It's not like this God dude was asking them to do anything hard.

Tim also imagined what the people of Noah's time really thought about him. Tim had tried to watch the movie about Noah with all the cool special effects but could not imagine talking rock people as being real. It was at that moment he figured the whole Bible was whack. However, now that he was reading the stories and the side notes, he was engrossed in its contents. He had considered just starting on page one and reading through, but he was having too much fun just flipping the pages and reading wherever he stopped.

He read about a king who made a baby with one of his general's wives and then pretty much sent him to his death. He was trying to figure out a modern-day soap opera to put that plot into. He read about some wild man talking craziness while wearing a potato sack while everyone listened. He read about another man who started teaching to adults when he was just thirteen. He was just randomly picking places to read and then trying to place them into a television show somehow.

One of Tim's favorite stories was about the family of brothers who sold the favorite brother into slavery and then later in life had to beg him for help. Tim thought, *Karma will get ya every time.*

It was going on midnight, and Tim had read several stories and comments. It was time for bed. His eyes were crossing from exhaustion, and he could audibly hear his pillow call his name.

Sitting on the edge of the bed, Tim reflected on the day's events and the fact that he fell asleep in the woods when it was too cold to fall asleep in the woods. He could not understand why he got so tired so fast and what all these voices were that he kept hearing. The one voice wasn't just in the woods, it would come whenever he started thinking about Mary. It was mind boggling and annoying at the same time. However, the other voice seemed to come in the quietness of his thoughts. Sometimes it was like a whisper, sometimes he could barely hear it, and then the other voice seemed to shout at him. It made no sense to him.

As he sat on the bed, he remembered when Tiny said his prayer and how genuine he was. How he had thanked his god for everything under the sun. He wondered who this god was that Tiny was talking to. Tim had heard other people talk about him but never really knew him or who he was. He did not *not* believe, but he really didn't actually believe. After all…what was the big deal if he believed or not?

Tim slid into bed and got comfortable. He decided that he would say a little prayer and thanked Tiny's god for waking him up and getting him back to the house safely. Tim then cuddled up in the warmth of his covers and mind and drifted off to sleep.

In his dreams, he remembered his grandmother and his mom going off by themselves every Sunday for a couple of hours. He never really knew what they were doing because he and his dad would go off on some grand adventure. They would either go to the woods, a trade show, work on a car, or just hang out. It was awesome.

The memories continued to flood his dreams. Tim focused on walking in the woods with his dad. It felt like Tim was only ten or twelve. They were walking along a path, and his dad told him to stay close. But being the boy that he was, he wanted to search out adventure on his own. After all, he was a big boy now. He was almost a man; he didn't need Dad to watch him all the time.

Tim let his dad get a little way ahead of him and then found a kind of hidden trail that looked cool to walk down. It was kind of covered over and hard to walk on, but it was awesome. He had his little knife that his dad had given him, and when he had to, he would cut vines out of his way. In the distance, he could hear what sounded like a party. He thought, how could there be a party out here? That's crazy. However, he was determined to find this party.

Tim continued to take off through the woods. The path was full of potholes and thick brush. Lots of adventurous complications to overcome. *It was great.* Nothing like that old people's path that his dad always walked. *This is what young men like to do…fight the wilderness.* Tim giggled in his head.

As he navigated one obstacle after another, he could hear the party getting louder and louder. He had to be getting close. It felt like he had cut his way through an entire county of vines and bushes;

his little knife was done for. He made a mental note that he had to sharpen it when he got home.

He was getting tired, and he was kind of curious why his dad was not yelling for him, but he was focused on finding this party.

Tim decided to take a load off and rest. He pulled a water bottle out of his pocket and got a drink. He looked around, and nothing looked familiar. Even where he had been was grown back over. It was almost like magic—like he was supposed to get lost. Tim began to get nervous because he could not hear his dad anymore. The party seemed to be very close, and he had *no* idea where he was. However, Tim was determined that he was going to make this happen, and then he would have a grand story to tell tonight when he got home.

Once he got his bearings on which way he wanted to go, he secured what was left of his water bottle in his pocket, and off he went. Pushing his way through the wilderness, the noise of the party grew louder and louder. Feeling a great accomplishment, he figured once he got to the party, they could tell him how to get home. At least he hoped so.

The noise of joyful singing and laughter was just on the other side of that grove of trees. Tim was getting excited. Pressing on, he pushed through the last wall of tree brush and could see a massive party in front of him. He went to go join them and found that he almost fell off a cliff and into a great chasm. Hanging on to the tree by reflex, Tim sighed a huge relief. He caught his breath and said, "This bites. I can see the party but can't get to it. What a—"

"Hey," came a voice from the other side.

"Hey," replied Tim.

"Come on over. We are having a great time," said the voice.

"How?" called Tim.

"Just use the bridge. It is easy. Come on."

Tim looked around and could not see a bridge anywhere.

"What bridge?" yelled Tim.

"Narrow one. Come on."

Tim searched and searched for a bridge that could safely take him across the chasm. That party looked phenomenal. He wanted to get to them. All he saw was a small board that looked like a two-by-four that was barely hanging on to each edge of the chasm. Surely there had to be a better way to get across. There was no way that little board was going to hold him, and as he looked at it, about three-quarters of the way over, there was another board that stretched out and attached to *nothing* but the two-by-four. Can we say I don't think so?

"I am going to find an easier way. That 'bridge' does not seem safe. Surely there is an area that I can maybe jump across down the way here," Tim called out to the person on the other side.

"Dude…I promise it is safe. That is how I got over here. Come on, you can trust me."

Tim thought, *I don't know you. Why would I trust you? And besides, that is a deep cavern.*

Tim took off down the edge of the valley in search of a narrower gap that he could just maybe jump over. The further he got away from the "bridge," the easier the path got. In his mind, he thought, *Now that I don't have to work so hard, I will be able to find a place to jump across. That bridge was scary.*

Tim was getting tired again. The chasm just kept getting larger and larger. There was no way he was going to jump across and get to that party. He was going to have to go back and chance that bridge. He decided he would walk a little further to see if he was just giving up too soon, and if he did not find anything within the next mile or so, he would go back and try the bridge.

Pushing on, the path was smooth and trouble free, but he was all alone. He did not know where he was. He did not know where his dad was. His mom was going to be furious if he was not home for dinner, and he wasn't even sure he could find his way out of this area. After about a mile, the chasm disappeared, and all there was, was the meadow in front of him. Even the trees were becoming sparse.

"Well, dang it. I have to turn around. At least I will have some easy walking for a little bit. I have been in this meadow for quite some time."

Tim sat down, drank the rest of water, adjusted his boots, and took off the way he came. It wasn't very long, and he found himself in the midst of thickets like there was no tomorrow. He wondered where they came from. He looked behind him, and the meadow was free and clear, but the path he wanted to take was going to be a bear. He could not figure out how it got so bad so fast when it wasn't like that before.

Not to be deterred, Tim knew he had to travel this path to (1) find the party and (2) to find his way home. Maybe he should have stayed with his dad. He giggled. Forcing his way through the overgrown area, Tim could hear the noises in the distance. He assumed it was the party, so he kept going. However, there was something not right about the noises he was hearing. They were the noises of wild animals.

Great, now I have to worry about getting eaten out here, he thought.

As Tim walked this path, the wild noises got louder and louder and scarier. Tim looked behind him, and it seemed like the meadow was following him, kind of like asking him to come back. That was weird. Tim was even more determined now to find the place where he was talking to the person on the other side. He figured that even if he did not join the party, he could probably find his way back to his dad who, by now, should be really ticked off that he did not stay with him and was looking for him. Tim was willing to take the butt whooping if it meant he was safe at home again.

The noises were especially intense now. It sounded like there were dozens of animals grinding their teeth and breathing heavily just waiting for their invitation to take him out and have a meal. Tim's nerves were jumping frantically as he made his way down the path of severe resistance. Pushing, tugging, and forcing his way through, he had decided that he was going to win somehow, some way, and if he were going to die, it wasn't going to be here where no one would ever find him. Using all the willpower and competitive motivation he could muster, Tim determined that he was going to make it home.

When he got past the extremely spooky noises, he could hear the party again. With a sigh of relief, he was feeling success. He was going to make it.

Ha! Can't touch this, he thought. Deciding to take a quick break, Tim rubbed his chin and felt whiskers. Confused, he looked in a small puddle beside him, and he now looked like he was eighteen. *Huh, that makes absolutely no sense.* Too tired to be worried about this, he figured he was just suffering from exhaustion and that his mind was playing tricks on him.

Up and going, Tim began to go towards the party noises again. The scary noises started to sound like they had started in pursuit of him again. The chasm was visible again, and the party noises were getting closer with each step he took. Not wanting to be devoured by whatever was starting to chase him, Tim picked up his pace. Not allowing any obstacle to keep him from the party, he pressed on until he could see the lights of the festivities.

The growling and gnarling sounds were gaining on him. Tim took off in a dead sprint through the remaining brush. He was not getting eaten today—not going to happen. As he got closer and closer to the bridge, he could hear the voices on the other side of the chasm cheering him on.

Come on…you can do it.
Get to the bridge and you will be safe.
Don't give up.
They won't follow you.
Keep going! You got this.
Get to the bridge… Get to the bridge…
Tim, we love you. Don't give up.

Tim stopped in his tracks. How did they know his name? The noises behind him stopped. Tim looked at the bridge. It looked even worse than before. There were holes in the wood now. Blood was everywhere.

The people continued to call on him to not stop—to continue across the bridge. But Tim was not feeling very safe or secure. The noises chasing him were silent, as if they had stopped. Tim sat down on a rock and stared across the chasm.

I am tired. I need rest. I am going to build me a little fire right here to keep the animals away, and I am going to take a nap. I should have stayed with Dad. He is going to be so mad at me.

Snuggled up on the ground, Tim went to sleep.

When Tim awoke, the fire was out. He could see the green and red eyes in the brush staring at him, waiting to see where he was going to go. It was almost as if they were going to leave him alone as long as he did not go to the bridge. The bridge was very close, and if those people really wanted to help him, why wouldn't they come over to this side of the chasm to help him with these animals? That made sense to him. If they really cared, they would come over here.

He reached into his pocket for his water bottle and found that it was full again. Puzzled, he drank it until it was half gone. He had been starving, but now he was full of life. Tim verified that the fire was completely out and would not cause any forest fires. He stretched and looked across the chasm at the party that was still going on. The bridge still looked unsafe, but he really wasn't feeling the love where he was sitting either.

The spans of the chasm seemed to shorten during his nap, so the bridge was not as long. He could smell the barbecue and was thinking that a good sandwich sounded very good. Unsure of how they knew his name, Tim took a little bit to weigh the options. As he sat staring at the lights, he began to hear their voices. They were no longer yelling. It was more like they were pleading.

"Tim, please come to us. Don't give up. You belong over here."

"Dad, please come back. Don't leave us."

"Tim, you can do it. Do not be afraid of the cross. It is your bridge."

"Dad, please, I am begging you…come home."

For some reason, they genuinely wanted him to cross the bridge. It made no sense to him, but he was starting to feel compelled to do so. As his insides felt the tug to cross, he could feel the darkness and the animals inch closer to him. When Tim got the sense that he was about to take a bite, he jumped and bolted for the bridge.

With all his might, he ran, and when he got to the edge, he stopped, took a deep breath, and then began to walk. "Are you sure it is safe?" he cried.

"Yes!" they all cheered. "You can do it."

Step by baby step, Tim walked like he was on a tightrope across the bridge. As he got closer to the board that was not secured to anything, he felt the bridge shake. The alpha animal was touching the end, making it shake. Tim stopped dead in his tracks. The area of the bridge he was at was soaked in blood. His traction was very slippery. The chasm below was very dark. Afraid to move any further, Tim closed his eyes and froze in place.

"Take my hand."

"Take my hand."

"Take my hand."

Tim opened his eyes, and there was a hand reaching for him. There was warmth and security all about him. None of this made any sense to Tim, but he felt like if he did not take the stranger's hand, he would definitely die. Tim cautiously reached out, and the hand pulled him to the other side of the chasm safely.

Once safely on the other side, the faces of the voices became clear. They were all of Tim's family. Love and security surrounded him. He was home.

7

"Tim, my love, please come back to me. I cannot think of living without you. Please wake up. God, please help Tim to wake up. Tim, I love you. Please do not leave me." Tears fell down Mary's face.

Tim stirred and opened his eyes. Above him stood his beloved wife Mary and all his children. Confused, he whispered, "Where am I?"

"Oh, God, you brought him back to me!" Mary cried. "Tim, you are in the hospital. You had an accident at the cabin. You were mowing, and a drunk driver hit you."

"But you were in an accident with Mom. A drunk driver killed you both," Tim replied. "I was all alone. I don't understand. What day is it? What day is it?" Tim cried.

"Honey, it is December 20. Your accident was September 10. You and I had an argument about going to church. Your mom picked me up, and we went without you. You decided to work in the yard, and when we got home, the ambulance had already been there, and the sheriff was there to bring us to the hospital. We have been here every day. You have been in a coma. At first, it was drug induced, but you started to show improvement around Thanksgiving but never came out it..." She paused to catch her breath and wipe the tears away from her eyes. "Your grandson was born on December 1, and he was—"

"Wait…my grandson?"

"Yes, your grandson. His name is Timothy Michael, after you. We decided to call him—"

"Tiny?"

"Yes? How did you know?"

"He and I built a birdhouse together and went for walks in the woods—never mind. I am tired," Tim said.

The doctor came in and shooed out everyone but Mary. They discussed what had happened, the treatments, the round-the-clock ups and downs. The doctor expressed that he had just about given up hope that Tim would wake up and that, at certain times, he thought that Tim would have to be put on life support.

The next few days, Tim was put through the wringer of tests to make sure everything was doing what it was supposed to do and if he was ready to go home.

On December 24, Tim was released from the hospital. The accident had only caused him to go into the deep coma from the head trauma. There were no other issues, and all test results came back free and clear of abnormalities. The ride home was quiet as Mary drove and Tim sat in the passenger seat staring out the window. He was deep in thought about everything that "he" went through while he was out. What about the voices? What about the affair? What about the chasm? What about the conversations he had with Tiny? What about the key? What about…what about everything?

Mary pulled into the drive and helped Tim into the house. The house was just as he remembered it. He cautiously walked around the house and found towers of pictures in the office Mary had built. They seemed to be categorized the same way he did in his coma. He walked outside and saw the unfinished projects that Mary had before the accident that he thought he had completed for her. It was all very confusing. The birdhouse was gone, but if Tiny was just a baby, then they could not have built a birdhouse.

"Tim," Mary said softly, "would you like a drink? A cup of coffee? Water? A shot of something" she said with a slight giggle.

"Coffee please, love. Coffee," he replied.

Tim found his way back into the kitchen and sat down at the breakfast nook. Mary poured his coffee and set it before him. She made herself a cup as well and sat down across from him.

"Tim," she started, "I love you. I am so glad you are home. I thought I had lost you."

Sipping his coffee, Tim was still processing everything that he had done but had not really done. He wasn't sure how to tell Mary and see if she could or would help him understand.

"Tim," she continued, "there were moments you spoke, and the things you said did not make a lot of sense. The doctors all said you were in a dream state of sorts and..." She paused. "You said something about an affair. The doctors said the words could be suppressed memories... I don't want to ask...but it..."

Mary could not bring herself to ask Tim about the affair. He had stopped sipping his coffee and looked at her deeply. "Mary... No, I never had an affair. But...in my 'dream,' you apparently did."

Puzzled, Mary inquired about what Tim could remember about his dream. He relayed that Tiny and him had become best pals and that there were several pictures of her with a key on a chain around her neck that he did not know where it came from, that the voices told him she had an affair with someone his mother had introduced her to. He told of getting lost and having to turn around and stay at Janey's on the roll-away bed. He spoke of the pictures being separated, finding Annabel's Bible, and reading the notes she left in the margins. He said that, after a while, he started reading the stories, and most of them did not make any sense to him.

Mary sat there quietly listening to Tim telling of his adventure within his mind. Tim became quiet for a moment, took a drink of his coffee, looked at Mary, and asked, "Who is he? Who did my mother introduce you to that you love more than me? The main voice I heard would tell me that our whole life together was a lie and that you loved someone more than me. If that is so, please tell me now."

"May I ask you a question first, please? Did you hear any other voices?"

"What does that have to do with my question, Mary? Who do you love more than me?"

"Tim...please answer my question. Was there another voice?"

"Yes, but they would only talk in whispers...except when I was trying to get over the bridge and that voice reached out his hand and told me he would help me." Tears were welling up in Tim's eyes. He could hear the echo of the other voice resonating in his mind, and the way that Mary was acting, the voice must have been correct. Why would she want to know about the other voice?

"Tim, do you love me?"

"Yes, I do. With all that I have. This hurts. Why are you toying with my emotions, Mary? Why?"

"Tim, the day you got hurt, we got into an argument. That argument had to do with going to church. Do you remember?"

"Not really, but if you say so."

"Anyway, I asked you to come to church with me. I wanted you to see why I go every Sunday. You went off on some wild rant about your time, your freedom, your this and your that. I tried to explain that it was not what you thought it was and to please come with me. I asked you, I pleaded with you, and you turned me down. And you turned me down harshly…" Mary paused and then continued. "Your mom picked me up, and we left. You were still tossing things here and there in the shop. For the first time, I was afraid to be near you. I did not think you would hurt me, but I was afraid there might be an accident and…so I chose to leave."

Mary sat across from Tim and watched how he was totally engrossed in her story. Then she continued. "While I was at church, I prayed for you. I prayed for you to see what I see. I prayed that God could reach you. I asked God to do whatever it took to reach you. So in a sense, you could say that I am to blame for you getting hurt. I asked the congregation to lift you up and help guide you to God. I felt that you needed what is called a 'covering of prayer.' The Bible says that where three or more are gathered in his name that—"

Tim interrupted. "He is there."

Mary's eyes lit up. Tim had never picked up a Bible, let alone read it.

"What does that mean?" Tim inquired. "He is there?"

"The first part of that is an instruction to believers that if just two people who believe in him (God) would pray to him about the same thing and believe that he will answer, then he (God) is with them, and their faith will bring forth his answer."

"Basically, your god just wants at least two people to believe he will do something for them at the same time?"

"Yes. If two people will pray the same prayer, God hears clearly the request."

"So I have another question," said Tim. "There was, somewhere, a speech or something that talked about three strands of rope being strong. What does that mean?"

"Simply put, if you have one string, you can pull on it and it will break. If you have two strings, you can pull on it longer and it will break. But…if you have three strings wound together, you will not break it easily. You will have to really use all your strength. The same goes for prayer warriors. If I pray by myself, Satan (the father of lies) can twist words and break your spirit, but if you have two or three or four or more, he is not going to break the bond or covering as easily. The more strands you have, the stronger you are."

Tim listened intently as Mary explained several of the stories he had read in Annabelle's Bible. As she spoke, she spoke softly and simply. She made the stories about things that Tim was familiar with, and then they started to make sense. By the time it was time for bed, it felt like they had discussed everything possible, but the "affair" still had not been discussed. It was late, and both of them were weary. It was time for bed.

Tim and Mary went to their bedroom and prepared for bed. Tim felt an urge to go to the office. In his "dream," he remembered where he had put the key necklace, and he wanted to know if it was there. No reason it should be, but what would it hurt? Tim walked into the office and turned on the light. Mary came out of the bath and stopped beside Tim.

"Honey, are you okay?"

"In my 'dream,' there was a key that Tiny gave me that you gave him. I placed that key in here. I am trying to remember where I put it to see if it is really there. Stupid, isn't it?"

"Not at all. Where did you put it, do you think?"

Tim looked around the room. It all looked remarkably similar to the setup he had done in his dream. As he slowly moved about the room, he scanned each inch carefully. When he came to the northeast corner, something shiny caught his eye. He moved towards that and found a picture of Annabelle. Draped on the silver picture frame was a gold-plated chain with a small Bible emblem attached. It kind of looked like a locket. He reached out and picked up the chain. With the Bible emblem caressed in the palm of his hand, Tim began to cry. Mary reached over to him and asked if he was all right.

Tim collapsed to the floor on his knees. Mary followed. She cried with him because she could tell that he was struggling. Tim looked at her and said, "This is the chain, but there is no key."

Mary took his hand that held the emblem and held it in both her hands. "Tim…" she cried, "the Bible is the key."

"What?"

"The Bible is the key to life. The key to happiness. The key to the One I love more than you, Jesus. God used our new grandson as a conduit to reach you. He knew that you would bond with your namesake. He knew that you would listen and want to help him. He knew that your grandson was the way to your heart. God is trying to reach you."

Holding on to each other, the two of them cried, Tim out of confusion and love for his wife, Mary because she could see God's mighty hand in reaching out to Tim.

"Tim, I did not have an 'affair' like you thought. That was Satan trying to lure you away. Satan knew that God was trying to reach you, and if he could make you believe that I had an affair and did not love you, you might not have ever come out of the coma. You would have spent eternity in hell. But you did not listen. You took your desire to find the meaning of the 'key' and your love for me and you came back to us. God used the accident to reach you."

Tim was a simple man. Simple facts were what he loved best. Cut and dry. Straight and narrow. As Mary explained the meaning of the stories and how God used them to reach Tim, it all was starting to make sense to him.

"Tim, God had to get your attention. You were so mad that day that nothing would have penetrated your wall. God allowed that drunk driver to hit you. He allowed you to go into a coma. He had to have your undivided attention. While in your coma, he took me away from you and gave you Tiny Tim. He used the 'key' as the catalyst to motivate you to seek the truth. All the while, Satan was feeding you with stories of mistrust and faithlessness to lure you away. You said that while you were walking in the woods, before you came back to us, you came upon a great chasm. The chasm was the choice for living or dying. As you made your way to the chasm, you faced many obstacles and fought your way through. You got scared when you saw the narrow bridge and wanted something easier. But all you found was an 'easy' open meadow, not an easier path to the other side. You said that when you decided to return to the bridge, you were followed by wild animals. Those were demons sent to scare you away from coming back to us. As you were on the bridge, you said it was covered in blood. That was the blood of Christ. You said you lost your balance and a hand reached out for you while the masses on the other side cheered you on. That was Jesus. Just as Peter sank in the water when he took his eyes off of him and Jesus pulled him from the sea, so did Jesus pull you across. And all you had to do was take his hand."

The boyish eyes of the eager young man sat before her, listening and weeping. It was all starting to make sense. Just as he had asked himself how the people of the Bible could be so stupid, he now was asking himself how he could be so stupid.

Sitting on the floor, the two continued to discuss the metaphoric principles of Tim's dream. At last look, it was after midnight when they finally made their way to the bed. The hour was late. They both were exhausted. Cozied up to one another, they agreed to speak again in the morning.

8

The snow was glistening about the yard and falling ever so gently from the sky. Snowflakes were gradually descending from above to cover the ground. Animals were scurrying through the snow in playful grandeur. Birds were swaying between the flakes as if dancing to a majestic song of peace.

Mary watched from the patio door to the deck. Sipping her coffee, she spoke to God.

"Oh, Lord, thank You for this day. It is so beautiful. You gave us the most precious gift of all—Your Son. I am so incredibly grateful. The view you have graced me with this beautiful Christmas morn is nothing short of a loving peaceful promise that you are in control and that you love me. The gleeful presence of the animals jovially prancing about the snow-covered yard and the graceful dancing throughout the sky eases my heart and my mind. It has been a rough year. Nothing seemed to be going as it should. I was so stressed. I was so worried about Janey and the complications with the pregnancy. But you came to her rescue on several occasions, and with the help of Margaret, Tiny Tim was born, healthy and full of life. I don't know how I would have made it over the last three months without Jon and Todd. They have kept this place up and running in their father's absence. Those two boys did not let anything get behind. You have truly blessed me. I want to thank you for Tim's mom, Martha. She has been my angel during these past few months. She has held me when I was crying and lifted me up when I was doubting. She showed me that you were with us. She never lost sight of your miracle. She never let me not see the different signs. The signs of your love. The signs of your compassion. The signs of your unfailing diligence to me and my family. She made sure that I did not miss a single moment. I could not be happier that you brought her into my life through her son. Thank you for guiding her in guiding me to you. You know already that my mom followed you very closely, but I fell away and didn't really ever look back…until Martha. You know our history. We argued and fought over just about everything, but somehow, someway, you found a way to bring us together. I could not say thank you enough. I do not think that I would have made it through without her shoulder and her strength. She is truly a pillar for your Kingdom."

Mary continued to sit in awe of the majestic winter scenery on this incredibly special Christmas day, reflecting on all the blessings that God had bestowed on her. She continued to pull pieces of time from her memory that stuck out predominantly and made sure that she made appropriate thanks for those gifts.

She finished her first cup of coffee and was about to get her second cup when she felt a sharp pain in her chest. It was like no other she had ever felt before. As she collapsed to the floor, the cup shattered and scattered. The noise of her hitting the floor and the breaking of the cup awoke Tim.

Like a shot, he ran into the front room, where he found Mary on the floor holding her chest. Crying out, "*Nooo!*" Tim held Mary in his arms, crying as he called for the ambulance.

"Tim," Mary whispered.

Tears flowing as he held his beloved, he said, "Yes."

"It's okay. God is in control. Please believe."

"Mary, please don't leave me."

"Tim, it's okay. Please, believe."

"Mary, I love you… Please don't leave me. I can't do this without you."

"Tim," Mary said softly as she drifted off.

The ambulance roared into the driveway. Jon, their son, was the driver today.

"Dad, what happened?

"I don't know. We were talking last night. She got up before me. I heard a crash and her hitting the floor. Jon…please…don't let her die."

"Dad, you have to let her go. Let these guys do their thing."

Tim released Mary to the floor. The paramedics began to work on her. Tim fell back and wept. Jon told his dad to get dressed quickly and that he would call Todd, who lived just a few minutes away, to come get him and take him to the hospital. Tim demanded to go in the ambulance, but Jon explained that that was not possible.

The paramedics worked on Mary and got her stable to transport. Jon called Todd, and Tim rushed into the bedroom to get dressed. By the time the ambulance was pulling out, Todd was pulling in and Tim was running outside to get into the car.

On the way to the hospital, Tim cried and asked God to please not take his Mary. That he just got her back. That he needed her. Their life journey was not complete. Tears flowed like rushing river waters. Todd had never seen his father cry like this. Pushing the limits of the car and the driving laws, they pulled into the emergency room. The front desk workers were aware of their impending arrival and quickly ushered them to a family waiting room.

Janey and Margaret arrived shortly after the boys. Jack stayed home to tend to the baby and Maggie. Martha asked her neighbor to bring her to the hospital. The family sat in the waiting room, quietly asking what had happened. Tim explained again what he could and that he was definitely scared.

When Martha walked in, Tim looked at her and asked her to help his Mary. Martha looked at her son and told him there wasn't anything *she* could do. She asked him what help he thought was in her power. Holding her son closely to her as he cried, Tim told of the conversation he and Mary had had the night before and that Mary had told him about how Martha had helped her get through the accident.

"Mom," he started, "please…whatever you can do…talk to God and ask him to bring my Mary back to me. Whatever it takes, Mom…please…"

Martha, with tears in her eyes, asked the kids to leave them alone for a few minutes to give their father a moment to gather himself. Without hesitation, they obeyed Martha's request.

Martha was a very prominent woman with a commanding presence. She was not large in size, but in presence, she made up for it. When she spoke, you listened. She was a very bold and upfront person who loved her family very much. Tim had been her challenge in life. They always seemed to be battling, and no matter what she did, it always seemed to bring a fight. Now, her little boy needed his mom and not an audience.

The children left as they were requested. Martha raised Tim's head, took her scarf, and wiped his face.

"Tim, I do not know why this is happening. I do know that God is here with us in this room. I know that Mary and I have been praying for you. We have been praying that God could reach you. You have been very distant from God since your dad fell in that culvert fifteen years ago while trying to cross a makeshift bridge to get away from something that was chasing him. He lost his footing and fell to his death. You turned your back on everything you were raised with. God is trying to reach you. He wants you to come back to Him. I don't know if that is why you got hit by the drunk and why you were in the coma, but it stands to reason. Do you remember anything about the accident?"

Stunned, Tim looked at his mother in disbelief. "How did you know what I saw when I was in a coma?"

"What do you mean, son?"

"I was walking in the woods with dad. We got separated when I went off on my own adventure. Eventually, I came to a great chasm, and there seemed to be a party on the other side. The people there wanted me to cross this rickety bridge that looked like a cross with nothing really holding it in place. I tried to find another way, more secure and safe, and found myself in a meadow far away from the party. But it wasn't where I wanted to be. I started to make my way back to the bridge, but I was being followed by wild animals. The thickets and brush seemed to build thicker and thicker, and I had to fight my way through them. When I got to the area of the bridge, the people on the other side were calling for me to join them, but the animals did not want me to. Finally, I got the courage to cross the bridge, but it was covered in blood. I almost fell, but a light with a hand reached out and grabbed me. They pulled me to the other side. Then I woke up here."

With a smile of pure love, Martha pulled her son close to her. "Tim, don't you see? That was God. He wants you to come back to him."

"Mom, why is this happening? Please help me. I am sorry. I am sorry I have not been the son I should have been."

Tap, tap, tap.

The door opened, and with the doctor, the kids came into the room.

"Doctor…please…Mary?"

"Tim, Mary is fine. We are not sure what happened, so we are running some tests. She is resting peacefully. We are not going to allow any visitors right now, but she did ask me to give you this."

The doctor handed Tim a gold chain with a Bible on it. Tim reached out and took the chain. His eyes were fixated on it as he heard each of the children asking specific questions and thanking the doctor. Tim looked at the doctor and asked if it was okay if he could just have a couple minutes, just two or three. He needed to see Mary. He needed to see with his own eyes. The doctor granted him a five-minute peek, but only Tim.

Carefully, Tim entered Mary's room. She was hooked up to a heart monitor, and they were giving her IV fluids.

"Mary, please open your eyes," Tim whispered.

Mary opened her eyes and gazed into his. "Tim, it's okay. God is with me. Please believe me."

"Mary, tell me what I am supposed to do," Tim cried. "I cannot lose you. Please tell me what I need to do. There are so many things going on that I do not understand. You are my love. You are my life. Tell me what I am supposed to do. Please…I beg you."

Mary reached out her hand and touched his. "Tim, all you need to do is believe." Mary drifted off to sleep.

Tears flowing down his face, Tim left the room and asked Todd to take him home. Martha told Todd that she needed a moment with him before they left the hospital. Martha looked at Tim and asked him to walk with her.

When Martha got the call, she immediately called Pastor Tom and filled him in on what she knew. He expressed that he would begin immediate prayers. After Tim went into the room, Martha and the kids said a prayer in a round robin-type circle. They lifted up Mary for a speedy recovery, and Martha claimed the promises of God that he was always there where two or more are gathered. She lifted up her son and asked that she and the kids be able to guide him.

Martha and Tim stepped off to the side, and she asked him if he would be willing to go with her to see a friend who may be able to answer his questions. Tim agreed. The two walked back to Todd, and Martha told him that he needed to take them to the church. Todd, without hesitation, said, "Yes, ma'am."

Tim's defiance to God started in his teen years but did not really go completely "south" until his father died in that accident. It was at that time that he completely blocked out anything and anyone who had to do with God. He would not even consider any possibility of his existence. Tim was in complete denial, and no one was going to change his mind. Because of this mindset, Martha and Tim's relationship was strained. When Tim and Mary met, Martha felt like Mary was pulling him even further away from God, and through her motherly protective strengths, she and Mary disagreed a lot. However, one day, God showed Martha her mistakes and found a common ground for her and Mary. After which, the bond was incredible. The two of them were a Godly force to be reckoned with, and they stood strong. The kids watched as they mended the hurt fences and fell in line with these two powerfully strong godly women. The battle then became to guide Tim. To show him that God was there and that Tim needed him. All had prayed the same payer—to do whatever it took to get Tim to come back to him.

Todd pulled into the church. Pastor Tom was at the doorway waiting on them. The three of them exited the car and approached the church. Tom shook Todd's hand and let him know that there was fresh coffee in the fellowship hall. He asked him to please get them all a cup. Todd nodded, and then Tom turned his attention to Tim and Martha.

"Good afternoon, Tim." Tom reached out his hand.

"Good afternoon, sir." Tim shook Tom's hand.

With a friendly hug, Tom greeted Martha. By then, Todd had returned with the coffee. "Would you two mind if Tim and I had a conversation?" The two agreed to remove themselves to another part of the church. Tim followed Tom to the sanctuary. Tom led Tim to a seat, and they sat down. They sipped their coffee in awkward silence. Tom could sense Tim was uneasy, and he could feel the enemy trying to work his way into this conversation before it even started.

"Tim, can I tell you a story that my dad used to tell me about a lady in his church years ago? It is kind of funny."

Bewildered by the request, Tim agreed.

"Well, he told me about this lady named Anne who used to take notes. She did not bring a notebook or anything, but she would take her Bible, and during each sermon, she would write notes about people in the margins. Dad used to sit behind her whenever he could so he could see who she was noting about this week. Dad told me this story once when he caught me writing notes in my Bible. He asked me what I was writing, and I would tell him about who I thought the passage was about. Dad quickly reminded me that each passage is about all of us. Oh, what was that woman's full name? Ann is all I can remember. But it will come to me. Dad told me once that, by the time of the sermon's end, she had written half her family in the margin with snarky comments."

Tim just sat there in silence and thought about Annabelle's Bible and how he thought the comments were pretty accurate.

Tom continued, "Dad told me that, one day, she left her Bible open, and someone read the notes, but instead of calling her out, they simply turned the pages to the Gospel of John, chapter 8, verse 7. 'Let he who is without sin cast the first stone.' Dad said she quit writing so many notes and started listening more. Changed her."

Tim looked at Tom and asked, "Why did you become a preacher?"

"Well, I could give you a big fancy answer, but the honest truth of the matter is I like to help people. And yes, there are many ways to help people, but I have found that this way is the best way for me to help them. I listen to the words and to the heart from the words. I hear the pain and offer answers as he provides them to me."

"Can you help me?

"I believe so, Tim. But are ready to be helped? That is the question to be answered."

Puzzled, Tim asked, "What do you mean?"

"Well," he started, "I can probably answer most of your questions, but are you willing to receive the answers? Are you ready to believe the unbelievable? Are you willing to accept the answers even if they are not what you want to hear? Healing is possible, but you need to want to be healed."

Tim drank some more of his coffee in silence and then asked if he could tell Tom a story. He said if he would listen to his story to the end, he would be listening to any answers that Tom could offer. Regardless of what they were. Tim said that he would sit in silence as Tom spoke if Tom would listen to his story. Tom agreed but asked Tim to wait just a minute while he fetched a second cup of coffee.

Lies. No one is going to believe you. This guy doesn't know you. I know you. This guy is going to tell you a fairy tale, and if you don't believe him, he is going to throw you out. These are very judgmental people. They don't care about anything other than their god. Your wife is dying, and you are here telling stories. You know that the doctor lied to you, right? Your wife is on her death bed, and you are here. What kind of husband are you? Leaving your wife to die alone. You are a sorry excuse of a man.

In the other room, Tom told Martha and Todd it was going to be a while and that, if they needed to leave, he would make sure that Tim got home okay. During their short talk, Tom felt an ugly presence in his church. A very unwelcome presence. A presence that was after Tim. A presence of evil. Quickly, he set Martha and Todd to prayer of covering. He reached for a Bible and asked them both to recite Psalm 91. They agreed. Tom left to return to Tim. Todd and Martha, not wanting to take any chances, texted the other kids and let them in on what Pastor Tom had asked. They all concurred to join in prayer.

"Hey, Tim, did you need a refill? I brought you one just in case. The breeze that blows through here sometimes sounds like the talking you hear in horror films. You know, the ones where some mysterious voice tells you to walk into the spooky house even though you know you shouldn't."

Tom handed Tim the coffee. Tim sat there in silence.

"So you have my undivided attention. I will listen to everything you want to tell me. No matter what. I will not judge you. I told you. I want to help you. I will not make fun of you. I will not think anything you say is crazy. I promise."

Tim nodded, trying to process what the whispers had said versus what the pastor had said. He was about to duck out of the agreement when he could hear Mary whisper, *Just believe.*

"Oh my goodness, I remember that lady's name. I am sorry...I know you were going to tell me a story...but you know when you all of a sudden remember something. Ha-ha, that lady that Dad told me about was a lady named Annabelle. Isn't it funny how that just came to me? So tell me your story."

Tim was floored by the pastor's recollection and that he had been, at least in his dream, reading that Bible. What were the coincidences that he would know that? Tim took that as a sign that he could trust Tom and began to tell him everything that he had dreamed about in the coma. While the two of them spoke in the sanctuary, Martha, Todd, and the rest of the family prayed, covering over Tim and Tom.

Hours passed, and Tom listened with compassion and understanding. They discussed what each situation meant and how God was using those times to reach out to Tim. Tom explained that God will use whatever method he deems necessary to get our attention, and it appeared that he was using Mary to guide Tim. Tom further explained that in his "dream," God made Baby Tim old enough to help guide him. That sometimes, adults will listen to a child but not another adult, so God made Tiny a small boy full of life and vigor and with a bond with his grandpa to withstand all time.

Tim listened with an open heart and receiving ears as Tom portrayed a loving Father seeking to find his lost son. No matter the cost. No matter the path. Whatever it took.

"Pastor Tom, I hear voices."

Don't tell him that... He will have you committed, and you will never see your family again.

With a commanding voice, Pastor Tom stood firm and spoke, "Be gone."

Tim looked at him and said, "Pastor?"

"Tim, God is after your soul. He wants you to give it to him freely. He will not take it from you. However, Satan wants your soul also. He knows that if you don't let God have it, he gets it for free. So he does whatever he has to do to keep it. The voices are his minions speaking to you. They twist words to make you think that no one will believe you. I believe you, Tim. You know when I went up to get us more coffee? I felt an evil presence in my church, and it was around you. They were talking to you then, weren't they?"

Tim nodded.

"Tim, the chain with the Bible (key) was the first clue God was after you. The chain had the Bible on it, but Satan changed it to a key. The 'affair' was between Jesus and Mary...to which is true. However, it is not the 'affair' Satan made it out to be. It is an affair of unconditional love. The walks in the woods with Little Tim were representative of you and your dad spending time together, the lessons he taught you on your walks, to set the stage for your walk with him in the dream to the great chasm. You noticed that as you approached the chasm, from each side, the path was narrow and difficult, but when you made it to the meadow, it was wide and easy. Satan wants you to believe that life is all easy if you take his way and that if you follow God, you have to battle for everything. That is not always the case. God protects you, guides you, and grooms you into his soldier. None of this is by accident, God is after you. He wants you back. Do you remember the story of the prodigal son? How his father allowed him to squander his inheritance, but when he returned, he had a party for him? God is waiting to have a party with you. He is pleading with you to turn away from Satan's ways and come home. He is showing you that life is precious and you need to cherish it not only here, but in eternity. Will you accept his hand, Tim? He is reaching out to you. He does not want you to fall into the pits of hell. Are you willing to accept him? Will you accept him, Tim?"

Tim and Tom talked into the night. Todd and Martha made more coffee and prayed. Mary cried in thanksgiving as she felt God's hand on Tim. By morning's light, Tim had agreed to repent and rededicate.

ABOUT THE AUTHOR

Karalee found a desire for writing at young age, but it did not really take off until later in years. Using her own life experiences, she began to put pen to paper in various forms of short stories, poetry, and devotional/inspirational writings. With encouragement from several family and friends, she endeavored to put her writings to print for others to enjoy. Following the guide of prayer and the Holy Spirit, *Chasm* was born.

CPSIA information can be obtained
at www.ICGtesting.com
Printed in the USA
LVHW032011130322
713178LV00001B/7